THE PLOT TO KILL HITLER

──── BOOK THREE ────

ESCAPE

ANDY MARINO

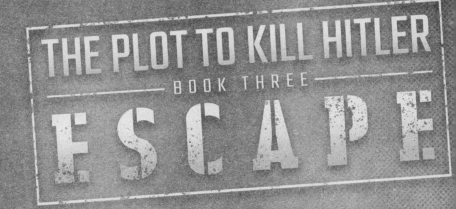

THE PLOT TO KILL HITLER

BOOK THREE

ESCAPE

ANDY MARINO

Scholastic Inc.

ISBN 978-1-338-35906-0

10 9 8 7 6 5 4 3 2 1   20 21 22 23 24

First edition, June 2020

Printed in the U.S.A.   40

Book design by Christopher Stengel

For Dan

THE PLOT TO KILL HITLER

BOOK THREE

ESCAPE

ANDY MARINO

ONE

Karl Hoffmann kept his back against the brick wall on the south side of the Gethsemane Church. At the other end of the street, headlights from two parked army cars lit up the Nazi checkpoint: half a dozen plainclothes Gestapo agents and a pair of SS men in helmets stopping pedestrian traffic and checking papers. Between the two military vehicles loomed a green minna, sinister and dark. Karl imagined the rough hands of those Gestapo pigs shoving Max inside the truck, pounding on the back door to alert the driver that he could take the prisoner to Prinz-Albrecht-Strasse and throw him in a cell.

As a surgeon, Karl had become immune to the parade of horrors the war visited upon the citizens of Berlin, but imagining Max a prisoner of the Nazis filled him with teeth-grinding dread. He stepped into a small fenced-in garden at the rear of the church, where linden trees sheltered a pair of wrought-iron benches.

"Herr Doktor Hoffmann." The low, polite voice came from the darkness off to his left.

Karl moved around the side of a tree. There was a slight woman slouching against the trunk. Her eyes were a pair of dull stones peeking out from beneath the short brim of her cloche hat. She reminded Karl of a theatrical tramp from one of Bertolt Brecht's plays, which he'd grown fond of during the 1920s and early 1930s. Before the Nazis rose to power and outlawed Brecht's work, of course.

"Ilse," he said. "Thank you for meeting me."

"You picked a fine night for it." Ilse lifted a small silver flask to her lips and took a long pull.

Karl knew that "Ilse" was not this woman's real name. Where she fit in Berlin's underground resistance network, he wasn't entirely sure. It was to Ilse that he had passed the vials of sulfuric acid that Colonel Stauffenberg had used for his bomb fuses. And it was Ilse who had persuaded the communists to make the weekly food drops in the back-yard of the Hoffmanns' safe house.

She could be a communist. A Jew living on false papers and borrowed time. Or someone like himself: a German doing what she could to resist the Nazis.

Either way, one telephone call to a switchboard opera-tor, a few coded phrases, and here she was—prompt, reliable Ilse. He wondered what her profession had been in the years before the war.

"Drink," she said, holding out the flask. It wasn't a question. Karl took the flask and poured schnapps down his throat. Instantly, the herbal bite of the alcohol warmed his chest and stomach.

"Thank you," he said, returning the flask. "Is it true, what they're saying about Hitler being alive?"

"Here's what I know," Ilse said. "There were actions planned for tonight. We were set to move against Nazi targets throughout Berlin, once the army began to arrest the SS and Gestapo agents. But we're standing down, because that hasn't happened." She shook her head. "Operation Valkyrie seems to be at a standstill. Whether that is because Hitler survives, or simply because Colonel Stauffenberg is losing control of the situation, we can't be sure."

The schnapps curdled in Karl's stomach. A cramp like a tight, heavy knot took hold. If the Gestapo and the SS were being neutralized, then maybe Max would have a chance. But if Valkyrie was headed for failure, the Nazis would strike back hard.

A boy caught firebombing a Hitler Youth building today, of all days, would not be treated leniently.

Karl clenched his fists as a bolt of white-hot anger surged through him. "How could Stauffenberg have failed? This was our one chance!"

"Keep your voice down," Ilse said.

"I'm sorry," Karl said, ashamed of his outburst. He

pushed his spectacles up the bridge of his nose. "I'm not myself."

That's an understatement, he thought. Every so often he would find himself marveling at the difference a few months could make. Last winter he had still been the head of the trauma surgery department at the university hospital, a man of steady competence who commanded respect from his colleagues and even from the Nazi administrators who tried to persuade him to join the Party. But just as the summer's poor diet had taken its toll on his body, the endless days cooped up in the safe house had worn away at his mind. He had always held desperation at bay, but now he could feel a frantic, nervous energy clawing at the edges of his awareness.

"My son is missing, and I fear he's been taken." He couldn't bring himself to say *by the Gestapo.* Ilse would know what he meant.

"We can find out if he's being held," she said, "but it will take time. We lost our eyes inside Prinz-Albrecht-Strasse, and after today things will be much more difficult."

Karl swallowed the lump in his throat. He had always been a practical man, but some part of him had clung to the hope that Ilse could work miracles.

"He's twelve years old," he said.

"I understand," Ilse said. "My youngest brother was thirteen."

Was, Karl thought. Ilse didn't have to say anything more.

"I'm sorry," Ilse said, reading the pain in his silence. "I didn't mean—"

"It's all right," Karl said. "I just can't accept that there's nothing I can do."

"That's the surgeon in you—always looking for a way to solve the problem. A little incision, a tube here, a snip there—but sometimes, as hard as it is, we have to accept that the best thing to do is nothing at all."

"And so I'm to leave my son in the hands of those animals?" He shook his head. "No. There must be *something*."

Ilse sighed. "Perhaps, if you weren't already a wanted fugitive with false papers, a known member of the Becker Circle, you could find some sympathetic official to plead your case with the Gestapo. But even if you were an upstanding Nazi Party member, it would still be difficult. Since you are an enemy of the Reich, attempting such a thing would be suicide."

"I could offer to trade myself for him."

"*Herr Doktor*, we're speaking of the Gestapo here. They will simply take you both."

Karl sighed. "You're right, Ilse. I'm sorry. I don't know what I expected of you tonight, of all nights."

Ilse put a hand on his shoulder. "What is expected of us tonight is changing by the minute, I'm afraid."

"So where does that leave me?"

"Do you want an honest answer?"

"I do."

"Take your wife, your daughter, and the Vogel girl, and get out of Berlin. I'm sure your son is a tough boy, but the Gestapo will sniff out what they want to know. It won't take them long to find your safe house."

Karl closed his eyes. Ilse was talking about the interrogation of his twelve-year-old son. Perhaps even his torture.

"It's not the kind of choice anyone should have to make," she continued, "and I'm truly sorry, but you do have to make it: your son, or your entire family."

He opened his eyes. "I've already told Ingrid and the girls to flee if I'm not back by midnight tonight. They know the contacts and the route."

"Good. Go home and join them, and don't wait until midnight. Berlin is no place for you anymore."

"I won't leave the city without Max."

There was a long silence. A procession of vehicles roared past the church. Karl and Ilse huddled close together, keeping the fat linden trunk between themselves and the street. They watched as a pair of the long, sleek Mercedes cars favored by SS officers turned the corner, followed by another green minna.

Checkpoints were popping up all over Prenzlauer Berg (and, undoubtedly, all over Berlin), sprouting like some fast-growing, insidious fungus to blanket the city. Ilse was right—the Hoffmanns shouldn't wait until midnight. If Valkyrie was sputtering into failure, things would get worse by the hour. Still, he tried to hold on to an ember of hope. Perhaps Max was just hiding out somewhere. Even if he was hurt, it would be better than being in the hands of the Gestapo.

Or perhaps Stauffenberg had succeeded and Hitler truly was dead. There was always a chance!

Ilse's soft voice brought him back to reality.

"You're a good man who has to make a bad choice. Whatever you decide, do it quickly. Don't let the Nazis make the choice for you."

Karl knew what was coming next. He could hear the *farewell* coursing through her words, the strain coupled with the steel of bitter resolve forged by years of permanent goodbyes.

"I'm afraid you won't be able to contact me again, Herr Doktor Hoffmann."

"I understand, Ilse."

She clasped his hands in her own, looked him in the eyes, and then she was gone.

TWO

As if in a dream, the headlights came slowly at first, oozing around corners. And then, all at once, Karl was surrounded like an RAF bomber caught in the web of searchlights that swept the sky above the city.

He had exited the little garden behind the church with no problem. It was only when he turned the corner at the end of the street that the net seemed to close around him. Heart pounding, he backed up against the facade of an apartment block. He was just one more anonymous citizen hurrying home—there was no way the Nazis could have tracked him to the church. And Ilse was highly skilled and very careful.

But he knew he was being naive. There were a hundred ways even a simple clandestine meeting could go wrong. The Gestapo could be tapping the switchboard he called to signal Ilse. They could have captured and turned a fellow resistance member who knew Ilse's whereabouts. Or they could have simply assigned a lucky agent to keep an eye on the Gethsemane Church.

You're just being paranoid, he told himself. He watched the cars screech to a halt—three Mercedes and a green minna, all of them angled toward the front stoop of a row house across the street from where Karl was standing. Doors opened, and half a dozen SS men trooped out and jogged up the steps. The lead man hammered a fist against the front door.

"Peter Weigel!" the man yelled. "Open up at once!"

When Peter Weigel did nothing of the sort, the lead SS man—an Obersturmführer, no doubt—turned and gave a quick wave in the direction of the green minna. The back doors of the vehicle burst open, and a pair of agents in long black leather coats hopped out. The SS men parted to clear a lane to the front door. The two agents carried between them a long metal cylinder, black as oil and shiny in the headlights. *Battering ram*, Karl thought. They paused at the door, swung the cylinder once, twice, and then smashed the door in.

Karl allowed himself a moment of relief that the operation wasn't targeting him, but this was short-lived. He couldn't help but imagine a similar scene unfolding on the front stoop of the safe house. *Karl Hoffmann, open up at once!*

He'd left Ingrid and the girls alone. And he'd failed to

find Max or discover anything about his son's whereabouts. Now he was adrift in a city on lockdown.

As the SS men poured into the row house with their pistols drawn, Karl moved quickly down the sidewalk. Ilse was right, of course. There was nothing he could do for Max. Getting his wife and the girls out of Berlin had to be his priority.

Tears came to his eyes. *Oh, Maxi.* He wasn't ready to think about his son in some horrible Gestapo interrogation room.

He would never be ready to think about that.

As he turned left, the dark streets seemed to haze, as if in a heat shimmer. He felt both light-headed and weak in the knees, abruptly swamped by the past. Max had been a colicky baby, and Karl had worked such odd hours in those days that he often found himself cradling his newborn son and pacing their Neukölln flat in the quiet hours just before dawn. The slightly milky scent of his son's face wafted down the dark street. Such a perfectly formed memory of the smell! Karl breathed deep. In the distance he could hear Max's odd little coo—a uniquely precious sound that Ingrid had dubbed his "morning chirp." Overcome by these visitations, Karl staggered onward a few more steps, then put out an arm to brace himself against the corner of an apartment block.

Some part of him knew that he was losing his mind, and

the levelheaded surgeon within admonished him to *move*. But the memories were coming faster now, a tidal wave of impressions, sights, and sounds of his son. His eyes blurred with tears. Bright lights cut through the haze, tiny dots in the distance. Karl nearly cried out as he was struck by a vision of his son as he should have been: untouched by endless war, untroubled by bombing raids and wrecked lives, going to school, playing soccer, growing into a fine young man . . .

Dear God, get hold of yourself! The voice was a whisper. It had no power to chase away these remarkably clear visions of Max as a well-fed, clean, happy boy, full of life and hope. And Karl didn't want to chase them away, did he? No. He wanted to live inside this other world—a world where he could keep Max safe like any father should. A world where he hadn't failed to protect him.

Karl thought he might be weeping. Light was all around him now, radiant beams swimming in the darkness.

Run, urged the voice, but it was still only a whisper.

Dark, brooding, ruined Berlin was a pencil sketch, a smeared background. Before him there was only light—so much light!—and Max as he once was, Max as he should be.

And then Berlin came rushing back. The apartment blocks asserted themselves, the streets drew themselves in, and the foreground of his vision was once again bricks, cobblestones, blacked-out streetlamps, and—

Cars.

A military truck, a green minna, a Mercedes. A parade of Nazi vehicles, coming from everywhere and nowhere, all at once.

Now the voice was loud and clear: *RUN.*

Karl obeyed. His first steps were halting. Then he found his footing. But there were so many cars, all of them screeching to a halt up and down the street. (Which street? Where was he?) Doors opened and shut, and the sidewalks were suddenly full of SS and Gestapo. Karl's fellow pedestrians looked stunned, squinting into the headlights. An elderly couple put their hands up in surrender.

He tried to clear his head, but it didn't make any sense. These checkpoints were so random, so sudden. It occurred to him that the Nazis probably weren't looking for anyone in particular—they were just unleashing their power and fury in the wake of the attempt on Hitler's life. Arrest first, ask questions later. Unless, of course, they simply guillotined you.

If only he could reach the end of the street! But now he was running in full view of the SS men taking positions directly in front of him. Everyone else on the street had stopped. That was the thing to do: reach casually into your pocket, present your papers for inspection, get your stamp, go about your business.

Karl stopped. He wiped the sweat from his brow.

It should have been simple. His forged identification was excellent. His composure was usually well kept. But his mind would not cooperate. He relied on the voice to tell him what to do and how to behave.

Get in line. He waited behind the elderly couple. They shuffled along. Just ahead, an SS man stood guard, raking the queue of trapped pedestrians with his eyes. His gaze settled on Karl. Next to the SS man, a short, stocky Gestapo agent in a long leather coat—despite the summer heat—made impatient hand gestures.

Papers, please.

Ahead of Karl, the old man rummaged inside a battered old satchel. He came up with a wooden figurine. Karl blinked. It was a knight on horseback. One of *Max's* wooden figurines. He rubbed his eyes, and the figurine hazed away. The old man presented his identification booklet to the Gestapo agent.

There had never been a wooden knight. Only papers. Karl took a deep breath. There, borne on the faint breeze, was the smell of his newborn son, lingering . . .

And then he was standing in front of the Gestapo agent.

"Papers, please," the agent said. His nose looked like it had been broken and reset. A fracture of the ethmoid bone, Karl's mind told him dully.

The SS man prodded him in the shoulder. "Produce your papers!"

Karl nodded. "Of course," he said, reaching into his pocket and handing over the forged booklet. The cover was printed with a swastika inside a circle, clutched in the talons of an eagle. There was a prominent letter *A* for *Aryan*, which marked him as an acceptable non-Jewish citizen of the Reich.

The Gestapo agent took it from his clammy grip. He opened the booklet. Inside was a real photograph of Karl Hoffmann. He was identified as "Wilhelm Fischer," born 1901, son of Otto and Agatha Fischer.

"Herr Fischer," the Gestapo agent said. He glanced from the photograph to Karl's face, then narrowed his eyes. "Getting some exercise this evening?"

Karl knew that sweat was beading on his upper lip, and he was most likely red-faced with exertion.

"Just running late, I'm afraid," he said.

"For what?"

"For an appointment."

"With whom?"

"A client. In Weissensee." He flashed a quick smile. "I'm an appraiser of antiques, and with so many items of great value coming into our possession from the territories of our expanding Reich, I'm very busy. As you can imagine."

He relaxed a little. The "Wilhelm Fischer" cover story flowed easily, and he spoke without hesitation. He held the Gestapo agent's gaze. The man's eyes were cold gray pools.

"You meet clients at night?"

Karl's smile turned rueful. "Between you and me—more than I'd like. Don't get me wrong, I'm grateful for their business, but some of my wealthier clients can be . . . rather demanding."

"I can imagine."

"They're accustomed to a certain standard of service, so"—he shrugged—"when they call, I come scurrying across the city."

The Gestapo agent gave a sympathetic sigh. "I suppose we've all got our masters."

Karl's pulse began to return to normal. This was just a routine interaction. Nothing out of the ordinary. Any second now, this man would stamp his booklet and send him on his way.

"Your wife must be quite irritated when you get called out so abruptly," the agent said.

Karl laughed. "I suppose she would be, if I had one."

"Ah. A bachelor *and* an appraiser of priceless antiques for our most distinguished citizens." The Gestapo agent glanced at the SS man, whose scowl seemed carved into his face. "Where did we go wrong in life, eh, Schulze?"

The SS man grunted.

The Gestapo agent smiled at Karl. "You must have quite

a few pretty *fräuleins* stashed away around the city."

Karl pretended to be slightly bashful. "Oh, I do okay in that regard."

The Gestapo agent's smile broadened, showing his perfect white teeth. "As understanding as she may be about your working hours, surely your wife draws the line at the pretty *fräuleins*."

Karl blinked. "I don't—"

"Ah, but of course you would keep them a secret!"

Karl shook his head. "I already told you, I'm not married."

The Gestapo agent waggled a finger and tut-tutted. "Herr Fischer, I'm disappointed in you."

Karl tried to keep his voice steady. "I'm afraid I don't know what you're talking about."

The Gestapo agent glanced at the SS man and smirked. "Herr Fischer, my friend. You're wearing a wedding ring."

Karl stared at his hand as if seeing it for the first time. His throat felt like it was closing. It had been years since he had removed his ring for any reason. It was simply a part of him, an extension of his skin. It hadn't occurred to him that "Wilhelm Fischer" wouldn't wear a ring.

"My Hannah, er, passed on, back in thirty-eight." He swallowed.

The Gestapo agent made a face of exaggerated sympathy. "How tragic! I'm so sorry to hear of poor Hannah's passing. How touching that you still wear your wedding ring as a tribute to your undying love."

Karl watched in despair as the Gestapo agent pocketed the "Wilhelm Fischer" ID booklet.

"This has been most interesting, Herr Fischer. I look forward to continuing our conversation at Prinz-Albrecht-Strasse."

Karl opened his mouth to protest, but before he could speak, Schulze took him roughly by the arm and marched him to the green minna.

"Papers, please," said the Gestapo agent to whoever was next in line behind Karl.

Another SS man opened the back doors of the boxy vehicle. Green minnas were tall, narrow trucks, and the oddness of their shape added to the feeling that to enter one was to enter a weird and unsettling new world. Inside, it was very dark. Karl could just make out two iron benches that ran the length of the interior from the rear doors to the partition that separated the prisoners' section from the driver's seat.

Schulze gave him a shove with a forearm across his back, and Karl staggered up the single step into the green minna.

"Sit," Schulze commanded. Numb with fear, Karl obeyed. What else could he do? As soon as he sat down, the second SS man clapped a metal ring around his left ankle and tightened it with a *clickclickclick*. The leg iron was attached by a chain to the bench.

It wasn't until the doors shut and he was alone in the dark that Karl was struck by the smell. It brought him back to the hospital's emergency room in the wake of a bombing attack: sour sweat, foul excretions, and behind it all the thick rusty odor of spilled blood.

He closed his eyes and focused his thoughts on Ingrid and the girls. Silently, he willed them out of the safe house. *Go now, my loves.*

He didn't know how long he would last in one of the Gestapo's interrogation rooms. He would try to stay strong, but what Ilse said was true: The Gestapo would find out what they wanted to know.

Everybody had their breaking point.

THREE

The Gestapo agent's name was Baumann. He sat in a chair across from Karl Hoffmann in a small window-less room in the bowels of "Alex"—the Gestapo prison at Prinz-Albrecht-Strasse. Without his hat and long leather coat to give his body a more angular shape, Baumann looked like he had been assembled from round lumps of clay. The muscles of his arms strained against his sleeves.

Karl had treated plenty of men like Baumann in the hospital. Street fighters and beer-hall brawlers. Men whose Saturday nights weren't complete without a bit of violence.

The only surprise was Baumann's perfect teeth, which made for an odd complement to his broken nose. Karl wondered if the Gestapo paid for its agents to have cosmetic dental work. He tried to quell his fear with small diversions—Baumann's teeth, a patch of peeling gray paint above the door, a chip in the corner of the table—but it was like trying to focus on a pretty sunset while your boat sank into the ocean. A laughable distraction.

Baumann set the "Wilhelm Fischer" ID booklet on the table between them. He opened it up and tapped the photograph.

"Who is this man, I wonder." He frowned. Then he looked up at Karl. "Any idea?"

Karl sat silently. Baumann regarded him without blinking. Then he picked up the ID booklet and pretended to study it in minute detail, as if he hadn't done so already.

"This is very good, you know. Much better than the junk we used to see back in forty-one and forty-two." He rubbed the corner of the paper between his thumb and forefinger. "The card stock is genuine." He examined the large red *A* printed on the cover. "The stamps appear to be real, too. You know what this reminds me of?"

Karl stared straight ahead.

"There was an industrialist—a tire manufacturer, I believe, though I could be mistaken. A certain Herr Trott."

Baumann paused. Karl struggled to keep his face perfectly composed, but his heart began to pound.

"Anyway," Baumann continued, "this Herr Trott churned out hundreds of fake identification cards in the basement of one of his factories. He had a whole printing operation squirreled away down there. And the work he was doing was magnificent. *Excellent* forgeries. Thoroughly impressive stuff. I have one framed in my office." Baumann chuckled and tossed the ID booklet back down on the table. "We guillotined Herr Trott in April." He frowned, deep in thought. "Or did we hang him with piano wire?" He shrugged. "We didn't waste a bullet on him, that's for sure."

Karl shifted in his seat. His throat was dry, his lips cracked. His last sip of water had been . . . when? Back at the safe house. How long ago was that? How long had he been in Gestapo custody? There was no way to tell time in this place, with no clocks or natural light. He hoped that Ingrid and the girls were long gone.

"I'm going to ask you some questions," Baumann said. "And I want you to keep in mind that I already know the answers. Why, then, you may be wondering, do I bother asking you? Perhaps you should consider that before you reply. Consider it very carefully. Now." He tapped the ink-scrawled "Wilhelm Fischer." "What is your real name?"

Karl pushed his spectacles up the bridge of his nose and then sat with his hands clasped in his lap.

Baumann sighed. He leaned back in his chair and rubbed his eyes. "I'm going to be honest with you. It's been a very long day. I'm sure you've heard the news about our Führer, may he live a thousand years. Because of that business, I'm afraid it's going to be a long night, a long day tomorrow, and then another long night. So let's skip the cat-and-mouse game and the sly evasions, and go straight to the part where you break. Does that sound good, Herr Doktor Hoffmann?"

At the sound of his name, Karl jolted in his chair. Baumann laughed.

"Our Swiss friend inside your Becker Circle, Hans Meier, gave us your name months ago, of course. And the university hospital keeps meticulous records of its staff. Your photograph has been on all of our desks since the winter, but you yourself have been a ghost." He shook his head. "I never expected you to walk into my checkpoint, but here we are. You know, the war is funny this way. My cousin wrote me a letter from Normandy. He's in the Second Panzer. He did a little schooling in Paris before the war and stayed in this little garret along the Seine. All very picturesque. He used to prowl the cafés and bistros in the company of his landlord's son, a young man named Laurent. Skip ahead to a few weeks ago, and my cousin tells me his unit is about to execute a few French partisans, when he realizes that one of them is his old pal Laurent! Out of all the little no-name French villages in the entire country, Laurent is hiding weapons for the French resistance in the one my cousin just happens to pass through. My cousin gave him a cigarette and a bit of brandy before he shot him. So you see, stranger things have happened."

Karl eyed the door behind Baumann. He wondered how many twisting hallways, how many sentries, how many locked gates, were between this cell and his son. Max could be right next door, and he would never know.

Baumann pursed his lips. He checked his wristwatch. "All right, Herr Doktor Hoffmann. Let's cut to the chase, as the Americans say. Here is what I will offer you. Tell us where your family is hiding. We will go there, and we will very gently take your wife and children into our custody. They will be sent to a camp—a *soft* camp. They won't be worked to the bone or gassed. They will simply be relocated until the war is finished. And best of all, you will know exactly where they are, and they will know that you are alive and well. You may exchange letters. How does that sound to you?"

Karl remained silent.

Baumann nodded. "I thought so. Let me describe the alternative for you. Continue to sit here in such brave and noble silence, and we will employ extreme interrogation methods. We are very good. You will talk. Our guests always talk in the end. When we find your wife and children this way, we will not be so gentle." Baumann leaned forward. "And, Herr Doktor Hoffmann, consider this very carefully—*you will never know what's happened to them.* Are they alive? Dead? In a camp in Poland? In a prison here in Berlin? Of course they will wonder the same about you. Is that the kind of father you wish to be? One who puts his family through an ordeal like that?"

Karl's mind whirled and spun. Was the location of the safe house one of the questions that Baumann already knew the answer to? If the Gestapo already knew about the house in Prenzlauer Berg, then it wouldn't matter if Karl talked. The walls of the room seemed to heave in and out as if they were breathing. It was very hot. Karl closed his eyes. It would be better for everyone if he told Baumann what he wanted to know, what he probably *already* knew. But surely it was a trick—Baumann was a Gestapo agent! There was no reason to trust him. Baumann's threat—*you will never know what's happened to them*—lodged in his mind like a splinter. He couldn't ignore it. Yet he couldn't just sit here silently, or he would be tortured. He had to tell this man *something*. But what?

He willed Ingrid and the girls to be far away from the safe house. Then he opened his eyes. Baumann sat across from him, arms folded across his chest.

Waiting.

FOUR

Max opened the cigar box where he kept the wooden miniatures that Uncle Friedrich had carved. He sifted through them until he came up with the knight on horseback. Then he placed the box on top of the pile of French theater programs—a gift to a future occupant of the safe house.

It occurred to him that the next person inside this room would probably be a Gestapo agent. The idea of some Nazi's hands all over the only keepsakes he'd brought from the villa in Dahlem made him sick, but there was nothing he could do about it now. Mutti had told him to pack only the bare necessities—a change of clothes, a few crumbly biscuits, a canteen for water. Everywhere he went, he shed pieces of the past. He stuffed the knight into his knapsack, took one last look at the tiny room, and headed downstairs.

Mutti, Gerta, and Kat were gathered in the living room with their bags packed. Papa's absence was heavy and ominous, like a strange new piece of furniture you could only see out of the corner of your eye.

"Can't we give him another hour?" Max said. He was convinced that as soon as they left the house, Papa would come home, and they would miss each other by minutes. That was simply how things went. Rotten luck lay over them all like a diseased blanket. He still couldn't believe that the Führer had lived. Did that mean that Stauffenberg was dead? Gone forever like Frau Becker, Herr Trott, General Vogel . . .

"It's already half past midnight," Mutti said. "We should be on our way."

Gerta plopped down on the couch. "I don't feel right, Mutti."

"Listen to me," Mutti said. "We're leaving the only city we've ever called home. Nothing's going to feel *right* about that. But we're going to stick together, and we're going to get through this. I promise you."

"No, Mutti," Gerta said, and Max noticed that his sister looked alarmingly pale. Strands of her wheat-colored hair were plastered to her damp forehead. "I mean I feel *sick*."

Mutti placed the back of her hand against Gerta's cheek, then her forehead. "Stomach? Throat?"

Gerta groaned. "I think it was those tomatoes we ate. They didn't look right."

"I ate those, too," Kat said.

"You've got a slight fever," Mutti said, gently but firmly, "which you're just going to have to deal with. When we get to the next safe house, you can rest."

"Uh-oh," Kat said, prodding her stomach.

"If they didn't look right, why did you eat them?" Mutti asked.

"Because we were hungry," Kat said.

"And none of our food ever looks right anyway," Gerta said.

"When we get to Switzerland, we'll have a feast," Mutti said. "I promise. Now *stand up* and follow me. Stay close, keep your mouths shut, and if you have to throw up . . . do it quietly."

"I don't even know which tomatoes you're talking about," Max said.

Three sharp taps on the back door made them all freeze. Max's heart leaped—*Papa!* But then he realized that Papa would have no reason to knock. He would simply use his key.

Mutti swore. "Out the front!" she said. "Quickly!"

"Karl!" the voice at the back door called out, followed by three more knocks. There was something familiar about the voice.

Halfway to the front door, Mutti paused, listening.

"Ingrid!" the voice called.

She was across the living room and down the back

hallway before Max realized who it was. He glanced at his sister and watched the same realization dawn on her pale, sweaty face. He listened to the back door open and close.

"Why aren't we running?" Kat said.

"Remember that shadow we told you about?" Max said.

Mutti came back into the living room, trailed by a tall man in a black leather jacket that hung to his ankles—the telltale sign of a Gestapo agent. His gaunt, hollow-eyed face was bisected by an ugly scar that ran from his forehead, across his nose, and down his cheek to his jaw. He wore black gloves and carried a small leather valise.

Kat gasped.

He had lost weight, and the scar was new, but the man was unmistakably—

"Albert!" Max cried out.

"Hello, Max," he said with a brisk nod. "Gerta. Lovely to see you again." Then, to Kat: "And you must be the famous Vogel girl. Pleased to make your acquaintance."

He turned to Mutti. "Ilse contacted me. She met with Karl earlier tonight."

Mutti grabbed the sleeve of Albert's jacket. "Then he's all right?"

"He was out looking for this one." Albert pointed at Max. "And now it seems they've switched places. If Karl's not here, then I'm afraid you know as much as I do about where he might be."

Max caught Gerta's eye. There was a greenish tint to her face.

Mutti dropped Albert's sleeve, folded her arms, and glanced at the clock on the wall.

"Ilse was concerned," Albert said. "And so am I. This place is no longer safe."

"We were waiting for Papa," Max said.

"I know," Albert said. "But now you must go."

"We were just leaving," Mutti said. "We're headed to the Klugers' for the night, and then—"

"Change of plans," Albert said. "The Klugers have been compromised. I'm taking you to Potsdam."

"*Potsdam*?" Mutti said. "Do the trains even run there anymore?"

Potsdam was a city about twenty kilometers southwest of Berlin. Max had been there once, before the war. Papa had taken Mutti, Max, and Gerta out on Fahrlander See in a rowboat that had sprung a leak. They had all rowed like mad to make it back to shore, sitting in a steadily rising pool of water.

"Don't worry about the trains," Albert said. "I'm driving."

Mutti hesitated. "If the Klugers have been compromised, then what of the Swiss route?"

"I'm afraid it's closed," Albert said. "But there is another way."

"To Switzerland?" Mutti said.

"Well," Albert said. "Not exactly. You'll be going somewhat . . . farther."

"Albert," Mutti said.

"You're going to Spain."

FIVE

As they followed Albert out the back door, through the yard, and down the alley behind the safe house, Max thought of the long black Mercedes in which Albert had chauffeured Frau Becker and the Hoffmanns. It was a fine car, and despite the circumstances, Max looked forward to seeing it again.

What he saw at the end of the alley was a green minna. Motioning for the Hoffmanns to stay back, Albert stepped out of the alley, looked both ways, and then quickly opened the back doors of the sinister vehicle.

"I'm not getting inside that thing," Kat announced, crossing her arms.

"Keep your voice down," Mutti said, "and *get in*."

Albert went to the front of the truck and settled into the driver's seat.

"They took my parents away in one of those," Kat said.

Max climbed the single high step and held out his hand to

help Gerta up. A moment later, Mutti joined them. It was very dark inside the maw of the green minna. A hopeless miasma hung in the air, the atmosphere stained with desperation and fear.

Kat waited at the edge of the alley.

"*Kat!*" Gerta hissed. "*Come on!*"

Kat shook her head. "I can't."

Max reached out for her. "We can't go without you, Kat."

"*Leave,*" she said miserably.

"No," Max said. "Families stick together."

He leaned out as far as he dared, stretching his arm to offer her his hand. She met his eyes. By the look on her face, Max thought that he'd finally done it—said the right thing to Kat Vogel. She hesitated another second, then let him pull her up into the vehicle. Mutti pulled the doors shut behind her, and they were plunged into complete darkness.

For a moment, there was silence. Then Albert knocked on the partition that separated the driver's seat from the holding cell in the back.

"Sit down, please!" Albert called, his voice muffled by the metal barrier. They took their places on the two iron benches that ran the length of the cell-on-wheels. Max and Gerta sat across from Kat and Mutti. The engine struggled to turn over, and Max quivered in his seat as the whole truck rattled and shook. The heady tang of petrol seeped into the air. Then the engine coughed, rumbled, and caught. Albert eased the vehicle forward.

Green minnas were not designed with the comfort of their passengers in mind, and Max felt every bump in the road. In a city as torn up and ravaged as Berlin, whose streets were pocked with craters, Max was forced to grip the edge of the bench while his body jolted and bounced.

Gerta spoke. She was sitting right next to him, yet her words were lost in the roar of the engine and the clanking of the leg irons attached to the bench.

"What?" Max yelled.

"I said I think I'm gonna be sick!"

"Just breathe!" Max said, praying that Gerta could hold down those questionable tomatoes. The stench in the back of the green minna was already bad enough—the thought of it mingling with his sister's vomit made him gag.

He closed his eyes and tried to calculate how long it would take to reach Potsdam. Before the war, they could be there in thirty minutes. But now? With the check-points and the mangled roadways, there was no telling how long it would take.

"Breathing's not working, Maxi!" Gerta said.

"Okay, okay," Max said, thinking quickly. He decided that she needed a distraction to take her mind off her cramping stomach. "Remember when you convinced me that the cave troll that lived in our old basement would only leave us in peace if I brought it little offerings of licorice?"

"Yes!" she said. "You used to leave this little pile of candy at the top of the stairs!"

"I always wondered about that!" Mutti said.

"I haven't had a piece of licorice since nineteen forty-one!" Max said.

"When we get to Spain," Mutti said, "you can have all the licorice you want! And Spanish licorice is the best in the world."

"Are you making that up?" Kat said.

"Yes!" Mutti said.

Suddenly, the green minna slowed and rumbled to a halt. Albert's voice came through the partition. It took a moment for Max to realize that Albert wasn't calling back to his passengers; he was talking to someone outside the truck.

Mutti didn't have to tell them to be quiet. If they'd just been stopped at a checkpoint, it would be up to Albert to talk his way through. Max wished there was a small vent or some other way to see what was going on outside. He imagined a squad of SS men surrounding the green minna. He tried to assure himself that it didn't matter—for all the Nazis knew, Albert was just another Gestapo agent on the prowl in the wake of the attempt on Hitler's life, hunting down suspects for interrogation.

Max strained to hear. A gruff voice outside said, "Prinz-Albert-Strasse is the other way."

"I'm not taking this lot to headquarters," Albert said. "Got something special planned for them over in Charlottenburg."

"I didn't know the Gestapo occupied such prime real estate."

"There's a lot our friends in the SS don't know about Gestapo business," Albert retorted.

Max remembered his father telling him that in Berlin, the Gestapo and the SS didn't always get along— in fact, they were sometimes at each other's throats, jockeying for favor with the Nazi high command. Still, he wondered if it was smart for Albert to antagonize the SS. He supposed he just had to trust that Albert knew what he was doing.

The SS man said something that Max couldn't make out.

"What is this, an interrogation?" Albert said. "Don't you have anything better to do?"

"We're doing our job, same as you. Now let's see that cargo."

"The Führer was almost assassinated today," Albert said. "And I don't answer to you or your boss. Now I'm going to start the engine, and you're going to move aside."

There was a loud *THUD* as the SS man slammed something against the side of the vehicle, right behind Max's head. The butt of a gun, maybe . . .

"Go ahead and scratch the paint," Albert said. "I'll be glad to send Reichsführer Himmler the bill."

"We can detain our friends in the Gestapo if they refuse to comply, you know."

"You're drunk. Get out of my way."

"What's your hurry?"

"Gestapo business."

"How about I ask our boss to call Prinz-Albert-Strasse to speak to *your* boss?"

There was a long pause. "All right," Albert said at last. "But I'm taking your names. This is going in my report."

Max heard the driver's-side door open and close. Footsteps approached the rear of the truck. A key entered the lock and turned. The back doors swung open. Max could just make out the silhouettes of two helmeted SS men, along with Albert standing just behind them.

Too late, he realized they should all be chained to the bench. What kind of Gestapo agent would leave his prisoners to move freely about the truck?

One of the SS men clicked on a small electric torch, and Max squinted into the glare.

The other SS man laughed. "Women and children! I'm sure our Führer will sleep more soundly knowing these dangerous subversives are off the street." He turned to Albert. "My apologies! Clearly the Gestapo is doing very important work tonight."

The light played along the partition for a moment, then stopped on Mutti's face. "What's a lovely lady like you done to get the Gestapo on your back?"

"That's classified," Albert said coldly.

The SS man snickered. His light roamed the interior and stopped when it illuminated the small pile of knapsacks and bags. "What do we have here, then?"

Albert was silent. Max tensed. He flashed to a memory of Albert sliding out of the shadows of the ruined opera house. He braced himself for an explosion of quick brutality.

"Well?" the SS man said.

At that moment, Gerta doubled over and spattered the floor of the green minna with the contents of her stomach.

The SS man lowered his torch and took a step back. "Dear God! That's disgusting." He turned back to Albert. "They're all yours, *inspector*. Get them out of here. And enjoy the rest of your evening."

Albert slammed the back doors, and Max was plunged into reeking darkness.

"Good thinking, Gerta," he said. Then he pulled his shirt up over his nose and mouth.

"Don't thank me, thank those communist tomatoes," Gerta said.

The engine sputtered and caught, and the truck lurched forward.

"I think I'm gonna be sick, too," Kat said miserably.

"Save it for the next checkpoint," Mutti said.

Max closed his eyes.

SIX

Two hours later, the green minna stopped. Max didn't care where they were—he had to get out of this truck. It crossed his mind that he would rather be back in the cellar of the bakery waiting for Heinrich to come chop off his toes. At least that place had smelled like bread.

The back doors opened, and Max jumped out into the night, gulping down fresh air. The others climbed out after him.

"Quickly!" Albert said. "In here."

Max hardly had time to get his bearings before Albert herded them all toward the door of a two-story row house. Max's heart sank. He knew they weren't on a sightseeing tour of Potsdam, but to be hastily deposited into yet another cramped and dismal flat was depressing.

They gathered on the small stoop while Albert banged his fist against the door—two quick knocks, a pause, then three more. A moment later the door swung open, and a pair of elderly women quickly ushered them into a dim corridor.

"I have to get that truck back to Berlin before the sun comes up," Albert said, with a note of urgency in his voice that Max had never heard before. "I'll be back to Potsdam as soon as I can get you new papers—hopefully no longer than a few days. In the meantime, Elke and Petra will take very good care of you." He turned to the two women and gave them a quick bow. "Ladies. Thank you."

There was so much that Max wanted to ask Albert. Had he been planning to kill those SS men before Gerta's sick stomach saved the day? Where on earth did he get a green minna? Was he going to look for Max's father when he got back to Berlin?

But after briefly clasping Mutti's hands in his own, Albert was gone.

Max turned his attention to their new hosts. Both women were at least Frau Becker's age. Despite the lateness of the hour, they were elegantly outfitted in long-sleeved collared dresses, one bird's-egg blue and one lime green, both cinched at the waist with flower-print sashes.

"My sister and I must apologize for the poor light in here," the woman in the blue dress said. She was slightly taller and more full-figured than her sister, and her hair was pulled back in a neat bun while her sister's hung to her shoulders. "Blackout conditions persist here as well as in

Berlin." She smiled, and her face became a map of creases and wrinkles. "I'm sure you're very tired after your drive. Let me show you to your room, and we can get acquainted in the morning."

The woman in the green dress nudged her sister with an elbow.

"Of course," the first sister said. "I'm Elke, and this is Petra."

Petra stepped forward, took Mutti's hand, and looked into her eyes. Then she did the same to Gerta, Kat, and Max. The skin of her palm felt odd, like crumpled paper with sharp corners. When Max pulled his hand away, he found that Petra had given him a small star made of meticulously folded paper. He glanced at Gerta. She was studying a small paper bird, holding it with a thumb and forefinger and turning it over. Kat frowned at a squirrel in her palm, while Mutti held what looked like a dog up to an electric light in a sconce on the wall.

Suddenly, Petra clucked her tongue, snatched the star from Max's hand, refolded one of its points, and gave it back.

"Thank you," Max said politely, unsure what to make of this whole exchange. Exhaustion troubled the edges of his vision, and for a moment he was convinced that he was dreaming.

"Please," Elke said, "this way."

Max hoisted his knapsack and followed Elke down a hallway decorated with small glass boxes affixed to the walls. Inside each box was another tiny object made from folded paper. The house smelled faintly of cinnamon, bringing him back to Christmases before the war, and coming downstairs to find Mutti in the kitchen baking *lebkuchen* while Papa lit the candles on the Advent wreath.

Thoughts of Papa swirled in his head, darkened by Max's certainty that if he hadn't gotten himself captured by the Hitler Youth, his father would be with them right now, following Elke down this strange corridor. Instead, they had left him behind in Berlin. What now of Mutti's insistence that the Hoffmanns were luckier than most? When would she start to believe that their luck was running out?

Elke led them into a small yet handsomely appointed living room. Shelves held a variety of hourglasses and clocks. On top of the radio was a curious sculpture—twists of braided paper in silver and gold, curling to form a gilded cage around a menagerie of paper animals. Petra shuffled over to the sculpture and used a long skinny piece of wood, like a teacher's pointer, to slide an elephant slightly closer to a turtle.

Gerta turned around and caught Max's eye. He shrugged. The members of the Becker Circle had been passionate, argumentative, devoted to the anti-Nazi cause. And Claus von Stauffenberg had been the epitome of confidence and poise. Elke and Petra seemed like the old ladies you read about in fairy tales who lived in houses made of candy. But if Albert trusted them, then Max supposed they must be committed members of the resistance.

Elke paused near a bookshelf full of musty old leather-bound volumes. Next to the bookshelf hung a small gilt-framed mirror. She slid the bottom right-hand corner of the mirror to one side, revealing a hollow in the wall. She reached inside the hollow. A moment later there was a soft *click*, and the bookshelf swung open like a door.

"You came to us at a good time," Elke said. "Our last guests moved on down the line, so we have a vacancy."

"Down the line?" Kat said.

"To a safe house closer to the French border," Elke explained. "The next stop on their journey to Spain. But we can speak of that in the morning. Now in you go."

Behind the bookshelf was a single windowless room. There were four narrow beds—*army cots*, Max thought. The rest of the furnishings consisted of a lamp sitting on a small round table, a dresser, and a mirror. One corner of the room was cordoned off by two thin sheets hanging from rods that protruded from the walls.

"The toilet is in there," Elke said, pointing to the hanging sheets.

"We have to stay in *here*?" Gerta said. "All of us?"

Max kept quiet, but he was thinking the same thing.

"Yes, Gerta," Mutti said wearily. "All of us." She turned to Elke. "I'm sorry. It's been a long night. Thank you for your hospitality."

"I regret that we can't accommodate you in a more comfortable part of our home," Elke said to Gerta. "But it will be much safer for you in here. Unwanted visitors are quite common in Potsdam these days, and I fear it will only get worse after the attempt on old Adolf's life. During the day you can come out to the living room, of course. But at night we must tuck you away."

Petra entered the room carrying a pitcher of water. She set the pitcher down on the dresser, opened the top drawer, and produced a tin of black-market biscuits—*English* biscuits, judging by the label.

"Thank you," Mutti said. Petra placed the tin next to the pitcher and left the room.

"Get some sleep," Elke said. "You're safe here."

With that, she went back out into the living room and shut the bookshelf behind her. The lamp on the table gave off a warm yellow glow, and the atmosphere in the room was cozy rather than oppressive, despite the lack of windows. A thick carpet covered the floor, and the cots were made up with fluffy pillows and tightly tucked sheets.

Max put his paper star inside his knapsack and set the bag down on the floor next to one of the cots. Then he went to the dresser and poured four glasses of water.

Kat chose the cot next to his and sat down. She bounced a little, and the springs squeaked. "It's funny," she said. "I'm exhausted, but I don't think I'll be able to sleep."

Gerta sprawled out on the third cot in the row and closed her eyes. "I'm not gonna have that problem."

Mutti placed the back of her hand against Gerta's forehead. "You still feel a little warm. How's your stomach?"

"Better," Gerta said. "I got it all out in the truck."

"Drink some water," Mutti said.

"Can't," Gerta said, turning over onto her side. "Sleeping."

Max handed a glass to Kat and another to Mutti. Then he went back to the dresser and opened the top drawer. There were a stack of folded sheets, another tin of biscuits, and a pair of spools with wooden handles. He reached for one of them and found that the two spools were actually attached. When he tried to pull them apart, he unfurled a long piece of paper crowded with tiny script he recognized as the Hebrew alphabet.

"Look at this," he said, holding it up.

"It's a miniature Torah scroll," Mutti said. "Elke and Petra are one of the links in the chain for smuggling Jews out of Germany. That's why they have this secret room."

As he stretched the scroll out on the dresser, poring over its remarkably neat script, he thought of the family that had been secreted away here before moving on "down the line." It seemed unlikely that they would have left this behind by mistake. He would never know, of course, but he chose to believe that they had left the scroll here on purpose, as a gift for the next family who sheltered at Elke and Petra's house. Carefully, he wound the paper back up and replaced the scroll in the drawer. Then he drained his water glass and sat down on his bed.

Next to him, Kat tapped out a skittering rhythm on the metal frame of the cot. Gerta snored lightly, fully clothed, on top of the sheets. Mutti went behind the partition and emerged after a moment wearing a long nightdress.

"Kat," she said wearily.

Kat's rhythm ceased. "Sorry," she said. "Didn't even realize I was doing it."

At the round table, Mutti stood with her hand on the lamp's switch. "Rest well, and sweet dreams, my loves."

The room went dark. Max took off his shoes, socks, and trousers, and slipped beneath his sheets. He stared up into the darkness, listening to Kat toss and turn. After a while she went quiet. Max's head throbbed where Heinrich had bashed him with the gun, sending pulsating waves through the pure blackness of the windowless room.

As Max drifted toward sleep, the throbbing waves took on the shapes of huddled figures—a whole procession of families displaced by the war, traveling through Elke and Petra's house, lying in these very beds, staring up into the darkness, obsessed with the details of their own journeys.

The dangers ahead. The fathers, mothers, brothers, and sisters left behind.

When Papa's face appeared, Max closed his eyes. The face remained, imprinted behind his eyelids. He thought he might never sleep. As if she could read his mind, Mutti began to hum Brahms's Lullaby, and eventually the faint and gentle melody carried him off.

SEVEN

Light splashed across a dark dream. Max opened his eyes. It took him a moment to remember where he was as he catalogued the unfamiliar sights—a table, a lamp, a wall with a big square piece missing, which shone brightly around the edges of a silhouetted figure.

Right. He was in the hidden room with its trick bookshelf. It was open now, and as the figure stepped forward, he sat up in bed.

"Good morning," Elke whispered. Max glanced to the side and saw that Kat, Gerta, and his mother were still asleep. "I've got breakfast waiting for you. Would you prefer tea, coffee, or cocoa?"

"Um," Max said, wiping away the crust in the corners of his eyes. "You have real cocoa here?"

"We do indeed. Come." She turned and left the room, leaving the bookshelf open.

Max couldn't remember the last time he'd tasted real

cocoa. How did these old women get such wonderful black-market goods?

He hopped out of bed, pulled on his trousers, and went out into the living room. Daylight filtered in through sheer curtains that hung over a pair of large windows, throwing bright shapes across the polished hardwood floor. Max looked at one of the many clocks on the shelves. It was almost noon. He had slept through the morning, which made sense—they had gone to bed very late. The cinnamon smell lingered. He followed Elke through an open door into a dining room where a crystal chandelier glittered above a long wooden table lacquered to a deep cherry red. Dangling from the chandelier was a menagerie of intricate paper birds.

"Sit," Elke said, setting down a tray on the table. "Eat."

Max sat down and she placed a steaming mug in front of him. He leaned into the steam and took a sniff. The cocoa smelled rich and genuine. Elke sat across from him and plucked a fluffy roll from the tray. Max's stomach growled. While his cocoa cooled, he made short work of a roll. Elke raised an eyebrow as he devoured it in three bites.

"Alas," she said, "we are short on real butter at the moment, and the ersatz stuff isn't worth feeding to a stray cat."

"It's okay," Max said with a mouth full of bread. "This is great."

He washed down a second roll with a sip of cocoa, warm and sweet.

"So," Elke said, folding her hands, "what should I call you, if you don't mind me asking?"

Max paused. Last night was a blur—Albert shuffling them inside the house, Elke and Petra ushering them off to bed in the secret room. They had never even introduced themselves.

"I'm Max," he said. "Then there's my sister, Gerta, and my mother, and . . ." He trailed off. "Our cousin, Kat Vogel."

"Well, Max," she said, "you're very brave to be making this journey."

He frowned. Stauffenberg was brave. Frau Becker was brave. He was just a boy who'd gotten himself captured, and because of that they'd been forced to flee and leave Papa behind in Berlin. The war swept him along according to its fiery, chaotic whims—the same as everyone else. There was nothing brave about it.

"I didn't really have a choice," he said.

"There is always a choice," Elke said. "And most of our fellow Germans made the choice to stand with the Nazis. Oh, sure, plenty of them are strong leaders, brilliant thinkers, excellent soldiers—courageous on the battlefield, perfectly willing to die for their country and all that. *But they have made the easy choice.* None of them are brave in the same way that you and your family are brave. Never forget that."

Max thought back to the person he'd been last year, when he'd envied the boys who got to play on the Hitler Youth soccer teams. It struck him that the only reason he had done anything to fight the Nazis—the dead drops for the Becker Circle, the vandalism of the Red Dragons—was because of the man who had died on their kitchen table in the middle of the bombing raid. After that, Mutti and Papa had made the choice to involve Max and Gerta in the resistance. But what if things had been different? What if Mutti and Papa had chosen to stand with the Nazis, like so many of their neighbors?

Then, Max thought, he would be strutting around in a crisp Hitler Youth uniform like Heinrich, and happily playing on a soccer team after school while the Nazis sent Jews, Roma, homosexuals, and other "undesirables" to the death camps by the millions.

He had never really considered this before, and it disturbed him greatly. The sweet taste of cocoa turned bitter on his tongue. He set down his mug.

"Is your drink okay?" Elke asked, studying his face.

"Yes, thank you," Max said.

"What's on your mind?"

He glanced over his shoulder. There was no sign of his mother or the girls. That was good—he hoped they would sleep for another hour. He didn't know why, but he felt more comfortable sharing his current thoughts with this old woman—a total stranger—than with anyone in his family.

"Maybe there was a choice," he said, "but my parents are the ones who made it. If they'd told me that the Nazis were right . . . I would have just become a Nazi."

"Perhaps," Elke said. "And perhaps if the Führer had devoted just a little bit more time to his painting, he would have been accepted to the Academy of Fine Arts and lived a quiet life in Vienna, and there would be an everlasting peace in Europe." She shrugged. "Or perhaps, whatever happened, he still would have found a way to fulfill his mad destiny. We can't look back on life's twists and turns and fret over some other path that never came to be."

Max thought for a moment. "So even if my parents were Nazis . . . maybe I still would have been *me*?"

"My point, Max, is that it's no use to admonish ourselves for the person we might have been, just as it's no use to pine for a world where things turned out differently. God grants us one life to live, and the good among us try to live it as best they can." She took a sip of her coffee. Then she sighed. "My son joined the Nazi Party in nineteen thirty-four, back when they were just a bunch of thugs and rabble-rousers in brown shirts. Nobody took them seriously. His father and I . . ." She shook her head. "We took him to the opera and the symphony, filled our home with books. We taught him to be a young man of the world. Growing up, it didn't matter to him that some of his friends were Jewish, or that his aunt Petra didn't hear very well or speak a word. But now, when he visits me, he sits in the living room and rambles on about a pure Germany cleansed of the Jewish influence, and he can barely bring himself to look at my sister. She's *mentally deficient*, you see. Useless to the glorious Thousand-Year Reich. Oh, yes, he brings me real cocoa, too. Which I save for the Jews who hide in my back room."

Max looked down at his mug. It was easy for Elke to tell him not to fret over a path that never came to be, but it wasn't like he could just flick a switch and turn off his thoughts. In fact, paths that never came to be were practically all he could think about right now. What if Stauffenberg's bomb had killed Hitler?

What if he hadn't gone out for one last mission with the Red Dragons and gotten himself captured?

What if Hans Meier had never joined the Becker Circle?

"I can see the sparrows nesting in your head," Elke said. "That's enough talk for one noonday breakfast, I think. Come and help me get some more rolls from the kitchen, and we'll see if we can wake the sleepyheads."

Max followed Elke into a small but very neat kitchen. Petra was standing next to the stove wearing a white apron over her dress, stirring a steaming pot with a wooden spoon. When Max walked in, Petra rested the spoon on the rim of the pot, wiped her hands on her apron, and reached up to open a cupboard. Inside was a single candle nestled in a small glass base. She lifted it out and set it down carefully on the counter next to the stove. Then she struck a match and held it to the wick. When she pulled the match away, the flame burned with icy blue radiance.

Astonished, Max went to examine the candle. It appeared normal, but inside the depths of its blue flame were brilliant flashes of crimson and gold.

Petra watched him expectantly.

"It's beautiful," he said. Petra smiled and went back to stirring whatever was in the pot on the stove.

"Where did you get it?" he asked Elke, hoping it wasn't some special Nazi trick candle her son had given her.

"Prague," she said, placing hot rolls on a silver tray. "It's very old and very special. My sister must like you very much. It's been a long time since she's shared it with anyone."

"Thank you," Max said. Petra leaned over and blew out the candle. A ribbon of smoke curled up to the ceiling and vanished.

Later, when Max tried to describe the candle to Gerta and Kat, he found that words completely escaped him.

EIGHT

lbert arrived at Elke and Petra's house the following
evening. He was still wearing his Gestapo disguise:
long leather coat, black gloves, vicious scar that
sliced across his face. He carried a large suitcase into the
living room, set it down on the sofa, and opened it up.

"Time to try on your new skins," he said.

"You brought us *skins*?" Kat said.

"No. I brought you clothes. But when you're wearing a
disguise, the clothes are only half of it. You can't just be a
kid playing dress-up. You've got to make yourself believe it
so fully that your skin believes it, too." He paused. "I can
give you the clothes. The skins are up to you."

He handed Mutti a neatly folded checked skirt and a
demure blouse with a button-up collar. Gerta and Kat
received identical outfits: long black skirts, short-sleeved
collared tops, and skinny black neckties.

The uniform of the League of German Girls.

Max knew what was coming before Albert took the next set of clothes out of the suitcase. A moment later, he found himself holding short pants that stopped just above his knee, a short-sleeved collared shirt, and a black necktie.

The uniform that Heinrich and the rest of the Hitler Youth wore.

"I would rather die than dress like one of those girls," Kat said. She tossed her new clothes on the sofa, folded her arms, and set her mouth in a defiant line.

"I'm *not* going to look like Magda Schmitz," Gerta said.

"Who's Magda Schmitz?" Max asked.

"The worst girl in my school. The absolute *worst*."

Mutti sighed. She looked at Albert and shrugged. Max was worried about his mother. Yesterday she had slept late into the afternoon, and seemed only half awake for the rest of the day. *I dreamed I passed your father in a car, going the opposite direction*, she'd told Max in a daze.

Albert seemed to sense that the moment was slipping beyond Ingrid Hoffmann's grasp.

"Listen to me," he said. "I am a high-ranking Gestapo agent named Klaus Bauer. My papers prove this, and they are impeccable. Your mother is my loyal wife, Renate, and you three are my picture-perfect children. Your papers also prove this. I am stationed in Paris, but I took my children to a youth rally in Berlin, and now we are returning. We visited relatives in Dortmund along the way."

He handed identification cards to Max, Gerta, and Kat. Max's card said his name was "Ernst Bauer."

"Why can't I be 'Max Bauer'?" he asked. It seemed easier to keep his first name. If some SS guard at a checkpoint called him Ernst, he would probably stare blankly before remembering who he was supposed to be.

"The Hoffmann family is on a list," Albert explained. "An 'Ingrid' traveling with a 'Max' and a 'Gerta' could raise alarm bells in an alert guard. Let us hope we only encounter the lazy kind."

" 'Ursula Bauer'?" Gerta said, studying her card.

"Could be worse," Kat said. "I'm 'Ingeborg.' "

"Put on your clothes and get used to your names," Albert said. "Practice calling each other by them. Get used to calling me 'Papa.' Remember what I said about your skins—until we get to the safe house in Paris, for the entire time we are on the road, you are loyal Nazis. Think of your classmates who were in the Hitler Youth. Act like them."

Max thought of Heinrich, and his father's knife flashed before his eyes.

"Now," Albert said, "try to get some rest. We're leaving at dawn." He turned to Kat. "I have some news for you."

Her eyes widened.

"Your mother has been moved from a camp in Poland."

"She's alive!" Kat exclaimed.

"Yes," Albert said. "And she's now being held at Ravensbrück. It's a camp for women about ninety kilometers north of Berlin. The Nazis are transporting their prisoners west as the Red Army advances."

Kat rushed forward and threw her arms around Albert. A stunned look passed across his face, then he patted her on the back.

She let him go. "Can you get a letter to her?"

"I can try," he said. "But you must write as if it will most certainly be intercepted and read. Don't say anything about your whereabouts—just that you are alive and well."

"I will!" Kat said. "I mean, I won't!" She put her hands on her head, started to walk to the back room, then stopped and turned to Elke and Petra, who had been watching the proceedings from the sofa. "Do you have paper? And a pen?"

"Yes, dear," Elke said. Petra reached into a brightly colored beaded bag at her side and produced a square piece of paper and a black pen with a smart silver cap.

Kat took the pen and paper and rushed away, calling out a hurried "Thanks!" over her shoulder.

"I guess I'll go practice my *Sieg Heil*-ing," Gerta said. She followed Kat into the room behind the bookshelf.

"This isn't so bad," Mutti said, holding up her blouse.

"Only the best for Renate Bauer," Albert said, closing the suitcase. "My wife won't be outdone by those stylish

Parisian women." He smiled at Mutti, but his smile abruptly faded. "I'm sorry, Ingrid. I didn't mean . . . they're just disguises, you understand. I would never presume . . ."

"It's okay, Albert," Mutti said. "Really." She blinked. "I mean, Klaus." She joined Gerta and Kat behind the bookshelf.

Max watched the awkward exchange with a strange tightness in his stomach. He was happy for Kat—it had been so long since she'd heard anything about her mother. The not-knowing was the worst feeling of all. Even the knowledge that she was in a place like Ravensbrück was better than wondering if she was alive or dead.

"Have you heard anything about my father?" he asked tentatively.

Albert stood very straight, suitcase in hand, long jacket draped over his forearm, looking every inch the Gestapo commander.

"No," he said. "I'm sorry."

Max swallowed. "It's okay."

Albert nodded and turned to go.

"Albert?" Max said. He didn't stop. "Um, Papa, I mean?"

Albert paused. "Yes, Ernst?"

"I don't know how to tie a tie. I never had to wear one to school."

"Oh," Albert said. "Do you want me to show you?"

Max hesitated. Papa had always promised to show him

one day. He handed Albert the long black fabric. "Could you just do it for me?"

Albert set down his suitcase and jacket and took the tie. He draped it over the back of his neck and made a few deft flips and turns of the fabric. Then he loosened the loop and handed it back to Max.

"Thanks," Max said. He couldn't bring himself to add *Papa*.

NINE

Max opened his eyes in darkness, shaken awake by Mutti's hand on his shoulder.

"Get dressed, Ernst. It's time to go."

Max rubbed his eyes. *Ernst.* What was his mother talking about? Was he still dreaming?

Lamplight washed over him, and he sat up. There were Gerta and Kat, dressed like upstanding members of the League of German Girls. Max had seen League girls arrayed in formation on the soccer fields near his school, and Gerta and Kat would fit right in. They looked like they were about to practice calisthenics. And there was Mutti in a fancy—but not glamorous—outfit, her hair tied back in a bun.

Now he was sure he was dreaming. He groaned, lay back down, pulled the covers over his head, and closed his eyes.

Mutti yanked the covers away. "Come on! Your father's waiting."

Papa! Max swung his legs over the side of the bed and stood up. Then his eyes swept across the Hitler Youth uniform he'd piled on top of his knapsack on the floor. The short-sleeved brown shirt, the half-length trousers, and the necktie with its premade loop. Reality crashed in. Papa was back in Berlin, whereabouts unknown. Albert was here in Potsdam, and Max was supposed to pretend to be his "son."

He waited until Mutti, Gerta, and Kat went out into the living room. Then he picked up the stiff trousers, the brown shirt, and the tie and tossed them onto his bed. He thought of what Albert had said about skins. It wasn't enough just to wear the clothes; he had to make himself *believe* that he was the loyal son of a fervent Nazi, a proud Hitler Youth boy. And yet he couldn't even bring himself to put on the trousers.

There was a knock on the side of the half-open bookshelf. Max turned to find Albert peeking in.

"Do you need help?"

"No," Max said.

"It's best if we leave before the sun comes up," Albert said.

"I'll be right there."

Albert went back into the living room.

Max took a deep breath and stared at the uniform. He told himself it was just stitches and fabric. It didn't mean anything. He could take it off and throw it away as soon as they got to Paris.

Put it on, Max. They're all waiting for you.

He tried to blank out his mind, but it was no use. As he stepped into the trousers and pulled them up, he thought of Heinrich, Gerhard, and the other boys of the Hitler Youth—thousands of them, all over the Third Reich—getting ready for their day in exactly the same manner. He thought of what he'd discussed with Elke—the queasy knowledge that, if things had gone slightly differently, he could have been one of those boys. How easy it would have been for Max to be the proud owner of one of these uniforms—not as a disguise, but as a badge of honor, worn to fit in with the ranks of his fellow Nazi youth. After all, these were the boys he'd grown up with, the friends and schoolmates whose parents preferred that they not draw attention to themselves or stand out, lest they be lumped in with the "relocated" Jews and other undesirables not fit to live in an Aryan society.

He buttoned his shirt and turned the collar up so he could tighten the loop of the necktie. In the mirror, he fussed with the knot until it sat snugly in the triangular space where the collar parted. He paused a moment to study his new persona. Then he vowed not to look in another mirror until he'd taken the uniform off. He shoved his things into his knapsack, trying to unsee the image of himself as a Hitler Youth boy—an image that would probably be etched in his mind for the rest of his life.

He did one final check in his bag for the wooden knight and the paper star, then stepped out into the living room. Gerta's eyes widened when she saw him. Kat seemed about to say something, but silenced herself and turned away. Mutti regarded him with placid understanding.

Only Albert—*Papa*, Max reminded himself—spoke.

"Fix your hair, Ernst," he said sternly. Max's hand went to the top of his head. He hadn't spent long enough in the mirror to notice his hair. It was mussed from sleeping. Mutti beckoned him closer.

"Let me," she said, smoothing his hair.

Max thought of all the boys in the Hitler Youth whose mothers fixed their hair before they went out marching and vandalizing Jewish businesses and whatever else they did.

Petra came from the kitchen bearing a tray of food. She went around to each of them in turn and solemnly handed over a roll and a small piece of cheese. She met Max's eyes and held his gaze, smiled, and then retreated back into the kitchen. As if they had planned their shifts, Elke appeared in the room as soon as her sister vanished. She folded her arms, studied each of her guests, then nodded her approval to Albert.

"Very good," she said.

"I'm parked just around the corner," Albert said. "I'm going to make sure that the street is safe, and then you can follow me to the car." He moved quickly down the hall and out the front door. Max stuffed the roll into his mouth.

"I'm very pleased I got to meet you all," Elke said.

"I'm afraid we don't have the means to thank you properly for your hospitality at the moment," Mutti said. "But after all this is over, perhaps . . ."

"Nonsense," Elke said. "You don't owe me anything." She embraced Mutti. "Safe travels," she said. Then she turned to Gerta and Kat. "Keep him in line, ladies," she added, pointing to Max. Then she joined her sister in the kitchen.

As he chewed his roll, Max was struck by the feeling that he would never see Elke or Petra again. How strange that so many people passed through the sisters' home, never to return. How many of them moved on down the line to safety? How many were caught and sent to the camps?

He took one last look at the living room, with its shelves full of clocks, its menagerie of paper creatures, and its false bookshelf. He wondered if Elke's son, the Nazi, would visit after they had left. The man would sit on the sofa and drink his genuine hot cocoa, never suspecting that a family of fugitives wanted by the Gestapo had just taken refuge in his mother's house.

"This stupid shirt itches," Kat said, scratching underneath her collar.

"I look like Magda Schmitz," Gerta said glumly.

"Max looks like he found his older brother's uniform and tried it on," Kat said.

"I don't care what I look like," Max said. "I'm taking this off as soon as we get to Paris." He turned to Mutti. "How long does it take to get to Paris?"

"A day and a night," Mutti said, "if we don't run into any problems. But we will."

She explained that the Reichsautobahn—the system of highways the Nazis were building across Central Europe to connect the farthest corners of the Reich—was limited to official traffic. They would be driving alongside Wehrmacht transports carrying troops, howitzers, airplane parts, and other material destined for the front lines. Albert would have to show a special pass at every checkpoint. And when they got to Paris, the Nazis' grip on the roads would become even tighter.

"Everywhere we go," she said, "we keep quiet, hand over our papers when asked, and let Albert"—she shook her head—"*Papa* do the talking."

Max heard the front door open and close. Albert appeared at the edge of the living room.

"Follow me," he said. "It's still dark, and the city is blacked out, so keep close."

Outside, Max took one last look at the sisters' neat row house. He thought he saw the curtains part in an upper room, but it was too dark to see if anyone was there, watching them go.

TEN

Klaus Bauer's car was a gleaming black Škoda with a silver grille and two spare tires that slotted into sleek teardrop-shaped curves in the chassis above the front wheels. Max had seen cars just like it all over Berlin. The Czech-made Škodas were favorites of the Gestapo.

"Where did you get this?" Max asked after they had piled into the spacious car—Albert in the driver's seat, Mutti next to him, Max sandwiched between Gerta and Kat in the back.

"A friend owed me a favor," Albert said in a tone that implied the topic was closed for discussion. He held down the starter button, and the engine came to life. Then he reached down by his leg, palmed the long silver gearshift lever that jutted up from the floor, and pushed it forward. After a light jolt, the car eased smoothly out into the empty street. Albert flicked a switch on a dashboard panel full of gauges, and the headlights lit up the predawn street. A man on a bicycle, clearly expecting to have the early morning hours to himself, swerved out of the way. Albert cursed under his breath.

Max supposed that running down a cyclist a block away from Elke and Petra's house would have been a disastrous beginning to the journey.

"We're off," Albert said. The dark streets blurred past. As if the atmosphere of the sleeping city had entered the car, no one spoke. Max tried to pick out familiar landmarks from his trip to Potsdam years ago, but there was nothing to see except a few early-bird shop owners tidying up their stores behind blue-lit windows.

Gradually a pale dawn crept across the sky, and a city took shape outside the car. Pedestrians began to hurry along the sidewalks, and a few other vehicles appeared on the roads. Max saw another black Škoda, several army trucks, and a staff car. Soon the buildings of Potsdam were behind them. They crossed an empty bridge, drove onto a heavily forested island, and joined a narrow road that sliced through the trees. Out the window, Max caught glimpses of a placid lake. It seemed like they were the only people on the island, and he was just getting used to this welcome sense of peace and solitude when Albert spoke.

"Have your papers ready."

Up ahead, the trees had been cleared. On either side of the road, parked among the barren stumps, were canvas-covered military trucks. Two uniformed SS men held German shepherds on short leashes. The dogs panted in the summer heat. Closer to the road was a small booth emblazoned with a red sign that said ACHTUNG—ATTENTION. A red-and-white-striped pole on a pedestal jutted out horizontally to block the road.

Albert shifted down and slowed the car to a crawl, making a complete stop a few meters in front of the blockade. A helmeted SS man jogged out from the booth and approached the driver's-side window. His eyes made a quick, darting appraisal of the car and its passengers, then he gave Albert a stiff-armed German greeting.

Albert rolled down the window. "Heil Hitler," he said in response. Then he handed over his identification papers and Reichsautobahn pass before the SS man had a chance to ask for them.

The SS man took the papers, glanced at the ID, looked at Albert, and then handed them back. "We don't get a lot of traffic through here at this time of day," he said. It sounded to Max like casual conversation. But Max knew that words could be used to set traps. And he remembered the last time Albert, in his Gestapo disguise, had squared off against the SS.

"I've been called back to Paris early," Albert said.

"Trouble?" the SS man said.

"The usual," Albert said. "We round up some Jews, the next day a Wehrmacht officer gets shot in a Métro station. Our spies in the resistance point fingers, and we put a bunch of French teenagers up against the wall for the crime. A month goes by, and we repeat the same charade."

The SS man looked wistful. "I was in Paris before the war. Degenerate, of course. But beautiful."

"We have corrected some of the degeneracy and sacrificed none of the beauty," Albert said.

A knock on the passenger-side window sent Max's heart into his throat. A second SS man he hadn't seen approach the car was motioning to Mutti to roll down her window. She complied.

The man leaned forward, sticking his head nearly inside the car. He had a long, horsey face and piercing blue eyes. "Papers, please," he said.

Mutti already had her papers in her hand, and she presented them to the man without a word.

Max had been distracted by Albert's exchange with the guard. While Gerta and Kat passed their papers up to Mutti in the front, he dug through his knapsack. Balled-up clothes, a few books, Petra's paper star, Uncle Friedrich's wooden knight—but no identification card. His heart beat wildly. He racked his brain—Albert had given it to him last night, and he was *sure* he'd packed it away. He retraced his steps in his mind. He'd put it in the pocket of his trousers, he was certain. Quickly, he pulled his wrinkled pants out of his knapsack.

"Ernst," Albert said sternly, turning toward the back seat, "I told you to have your papers ready. These men don't have all day."

"Yes, Papa. I'm sorry."

Max pulled his crumpled identification card from the pocket, smoothed it as best he could, and handed it to Mutti, who smoothed it some more and passed it to the guard.

Max noticed that his hand was trembling. He also noticed that the SS man at Albert's window was regarding him with interest.

"What happened to your face?" he asked through the window.

Startled, Max's mind went blank. *My face?* Then he realized the guard must be referring to the bruise that remained from Heinrich's pistol cracking his skull.

"I play goalie on my soccer team," he said, hoping that would be explanation enough.

The SS man smiled. "Using your head, I see."

Max tried to look bold. "Whatever gets the save."

The guard gestured to a third man inside the booth, who stepped out and lifted the barricade so that the pole pointed at the sky.

The second SS man handed the identification cards back to Mutti. After another exchange of *Heil Hitlers*, Albert rolled up his window, put the car into drive, and drove through the open gate.

"Ernst," he said as they sped away down the forest trail, "the next time I tell you to have your papers ready, please *have your papers ready*."

"Yes, Papa," Max said.

"Papa," Kat said, "what would you do if they made us step out of the car?"

Max reminded himself that Kat hadn't seen Albert dispatch those Gestapo agents in the ruins of the opera house.

"Shoot them," Albert said matter-of-factly. "Eventually we'd have to leave the car behind—it's too easy to tail—and then we'd cross Germany on foot, traveling at night, sleeping in barns, eating whatever we find."

"Let's hope it doesn't come to that," Mutti said.

"I don't have the proper shoes," Kat said.

"Ernst," Gerta said, "for God's sake, have your papers ready next time."

ELEVEN

The German countryside swept past the windows in a hundred shades of green. The Reichsautobahn cut through rolling hills, twin highways divided by a grassy strip that sprouted tentative foliage here and there like a poorly shaved head. Max dozed fitfully in the back seat and woke to flashes of scenery that he would later be unable to differentiate from dreams—a fairy-tale castle on a distant hill, its gables stretching to challenge the low clouds. Hidden Luftwaffe fighter planes tucked into trees alongside the highway, their snub noses poking from the greenery. Bridges arched like Roman aqueducts hung with silver eagles gripping swastikas in their talons.

They passed few fellow travelers, and there were long stretches where it felt like the Škoda was the only vehicle on the road in all of Germany. Staring out at the endless forests dotted with the alabaster stones of ancient villages, chimney smoke curling up into the sky, it was easy to forget that they were fleeing the epicenter of a five-year war that had pulled in most of the world. But all it took to snap him back to reality was for Max to spy Albert's leather-gloved hands on the steering wheel.

One thought in particular troubled him the most: Every kilometer carried them farther away from Papa.

He dozed for a while. Sometime later he woke with Gerta's head on his shoulder, squirmed a little in his seat, and went back to sleep.

He woke again during the late afternoon when the sun was on its downward plunge. The car had slowed. There was traffic here—canvas-covered Wehrmacht trucks, convertible cars driven by uniformed soldiers in goggles, even a procession of Panzer tanks crawling along like armored beetles.

Out the right-hand window—*north*, Max guessed—a city like a low gray ash heap came into view. Distant ruins hazed into an unbroken carpet of dull slag, punctuated by a cathedral's Gothic spires that presided over the wrecked landscape.

"Frankfurt," Mutti announced. Max had never been to Frankfurt, but he could imagine that before the war it must have been as grand as Berlin. A river curled like the Spree, a sparkling blue line snaking through the ruins. He had heard about the bombing of cities all across Germany, of course, and he had seen the hollow-eyed refugees from

Hamburg who had poured into Berlin by the thousands.

If only Stauffenberg had succeeded! Hitler, it seemed, would never give up. The Führer would rather see all of Germany reduced to dust than surrender. Max wondered if there would even be a Berlin to go back to after the war ended.

The checkpoints on the roads just south of Frankfurt were much different than the small hut manned by a handful of guards in the woods outside of Potsdam. A concrete blockhouse squatted on the side of the road, emblazoned with the SS insignia. There were at least a dozen men milling about, and Max counted five well-fed German shepherds, much healthier than the mangy strays that roamed Berlin. The SS guards carried rifles slung over their shoulders, and the long barrel of a machine gun jutted from its nest atop the blockhouse.

This time, Max had his papers ready, and the car was waved through after what felt like a cursory glance. As they drove away, Albert explained.

"We've practically joined this Wehrmacht convoy headed for the Siegfried line," he said, indicating the parade of military vehicles that stretched along the highway in front of and behind the Škoda. "The guards probably assume that nobody's stupid enough to be fleeing Germany this way."

"Good thing *we're* that stupid," Kat said.

"What's the Siegfried line?" Gerta asked.

"Hitler's reinforcing German positions along the French border, and the Siegfried line is full of old bunkers and gun emplacements and tank traps from the First World War. Even the Führer has to admit that the Allies will be there before long."

"Are we going to get caught in the fighting?" Max asked.

"They're not there yet," Mutti said.

"The funny thing about the border," Albert said, "is that it doesn't really exist anymore, ever since Hitler annexed Alsace-Lorraine. All that French territory is part of the Reich now. So we're not really 'crossing over' into France— the Reich just keeps going and going. The people in this part of it just happen to speak French. At least that's how the Nazis think of it."

"Max can translate for us," Gerta said. "As long as it's a conversation about French theater."

"*Oui,*" Max said. Albert's words echoed inside his head. *The Reich just keeps going and going.* At the beginning of the war, all these European borders became elastic, stretched out by the advancing Wehrmacht from the English Channel to Russia's vast, frigid interior. But now the borders were snapping back into place as the Allies advanced in the west and the Red Army in the east. And yet the borders weren't snapping back fast enough to save Kat's mother, or Papa, or anyone else stuck in Germany. Hitler was desperate to hold on to what he'd gained, even if he had to claw at scraps of territory until they were shredded bits of what they had been.

The promise of night seemed to hover about the car, and then darkness fell so quickly that Max wondered if he'd dozed off again. The Reichsautobahn was reduced to the gray pavement caught in the Škoda's headlights, and they drove steadily onward, a lighted bubble in a dark land. Occasionally they passed sluggish flatbed trucks crawling along, laden with a hundred tons of machinery.

Eventually, traffic funneled dutifully into the queue of another checkpoint lit by rows of bright bulbs on steel racks that resembled the framework of the Red Army's *Katyusha* rocket launcher.

Papers, please.

Until they reached this checkpoint, the SS guards had been young and strong. But this man was much older, and he walked with a slight limp. His bespectacled face was doughy and soft. It was as if he'd just been yanked from his armchair, where he'd been smoking a pipe and reading a book, thrust into an SS uniform, and sent off to the French border territory of Alsace-Lorraine.

He studied their identification cards for a very long time. Then he asked Albert politely if he wouldn't mind stepping out of the car.

Max tensed. This checkpoint was huge—there were

several lanes of vehicles, and at least two dozen guards. Not to mention the German shepherds, a pair of machine-gun emplacements, and a thick striped barrier—ACHTUNG. It wasn't some isolated posting in the woods. Albert would be cut down before he could draw his gun, and then the rest of them would be dragged from the car and hauled back to Germany. If they weren't simply killed in the crossfire.

"Is there a problem?" Albert said.

The SS man sighed. "If I'm being honest, I have a quota to fill. I'll need to run a formal check on your papers."

"I see," Albert said. "The problem is, I'm due back in Paris immediately, and I don't have time to wait for you to call this in. So. I propose we come to some sort of arrangement and settle this immediately."

He reached into his pocket and produced a thick roll of Reichsmarks. The SS man glanced over his shoulder at the concrete blockhouse on the side of the highway, then turned back to Albert. He leaned close to the open window and kept his voice low.

"We both know those will be worthless in a few months."

Mutti stretched her arm across the front seat and held out a silver bracelet. Max recognized it as the one Papa had given her on their anniversary in the last year before the war.

Wordlessly, Albert took the bracelet and handed it to the

SS man, who closed one eye and examined it closely for a moment. Then he slid it into his pocket.

"Move along." He stepped back from the car and waved to the blockhouse. The barrier went up. Albert shifted, and the car eased forward, and they put the checkpoint behind them.

"Thank you, Renate," Albert said after a long silence.

"Karl would have wanted me to put it to good use," she said.

"That guy was the oldest soldier I've ever seen," Max said.

Albert laughed. "That's because all the young ones who spent the war occupying France have been transferred to the Eastern Front. They went from the cushiest job in the Reich—hanging around the cafés in Paris—to the most miserable posting in the world."

Albert didn't sound like he sympathized. Max settled back against the seat, keeping an eye out for anything remotely interesting in the wooded darkness of eastern France. All he saw were some road signs in French, along with a few hastily posted signs for the German occupiers, pointing out the way to Paris.

Traffic was thin. The Škoda ate up the highway. After a while, Albert slowed and pulled off onto a bumpy cobblestone path that was clearly not meant for an automobile.

"We'll stop here for the night," he announced. Max

was about to ask him where exactly *here* was, when the path took a sharp turn up a slight incline and the headlights moved across a row of tightly packed cottages. They were the color of creamy confections, topped with chimneys and shingled rooftops. Neat shutters of pale green and blue covered the windows.

There was something different about this little village, something Max couldn't quite put his finger on. For the first time since they'd crossed the border, he felt like he was truly in France.

The street was empty. Albert eased the car slowly past a narrow bridge, across a thin trickle of a stream, then came to a stop in front of a large stone house with a pair of chimneys. The brick stacks rose from opposite ends of the roof. A sign above the door said AUBERGE.

"It's an inn," Max said, recognizing the word.

"I hope they have a room," Gerta said. "I'm so tired of sitting up in this seat."

"Oh, I wouldn't worry," Albert said grimly. "They'll have a room for us." Max understood what he meant. A village in occupied France had better show some hospitality to a high-ranking Gestapo agent and his family.

A moment later, they were all stretching their legs outside the car. Max's body felt coiled and stiff. Kat put her hands on her hips and leaned back. Max winced as the bones in her back audibly cracked.

Inside the *auberge*, there was a small anteroom with a pair of worn leather chairs and a desk with a stack of papers and a silver bell. Albert brought his palm down on the bell, and a shrill chime rang out. A moment later, a young woman in a sauce-stained apron came bustling through a swinging door. The smile on her face faded as soon as she saw her new guests, but she replaced it in a flash—except now it looked strained.

"Hello," she said in heavily accented German. "I am Adele. I am sorry, but my German is not good."

Albert replied in rapid French. Her eyes widened. She wiped her hands on her apron and hurried behind the desk. Max tried to make out what Albert was saying, but he spoke too fast. Still, he was able to catch a few basic words: *hungry, tired, food, room.*

Adele replied in what sounded to Max like total gibberish. He was completely lost. Reading a few theater programs had not prepared him for the reality of the spoken language. She gestured toward the swinging door and fixed another strained smile to her face.

Albert turned to the Hoffmanns and Kat.

"The restaurant is closed, but she will make us some food. After that, we will have a pair of adjoining rooms. And hot water."

Adele called out *"Colette!"* and a moment later a girl burst through the swinging door. She was about Max's age, with a high forehead, delicate features, and severely straight raven-colored hair. She took one look at the new guests and her expression curdled into pure disgust. Then she caught herself and gave a slight bow. Before she went to speak to her mother, she snuck another glance and met Max's eyes. She jutted her chin out slightly, and the mixture of fear and defiance in her face made him turn away in shame. He felt his forehead getting warm, and he knew his cheeks were flushed. He could feel every fiber and stitch of the Hitler Youth uniform. He wanted to shout at the girl Colette—*this isn't me, it's just a disguise. I hate the Nazis as much as you do!* He could feel the words on the tip of his tongue, and for a single reckless moment, he teetered on the edge of actually opening his mouth. But he forced himself under control. He would leave this village in the morning and never see these people again—who cared what they thought of him?

And yet, as Colette beckoned for them all to follow her through the swinging door, Max's shame clawed at his mind. The way the girl and her mother looked at Albert— and at Max—made it easy to see the revulsion churning beneath their polite and deferential demeanors. What had the Nazi occupiers done to the people of this village? Had the men been killed or sent away to the camps?

As Colette led them into a small dining room decorated like a hunting lodge, with mounted antlers jutting from the wall and exposed beams crossing the peaked ceiling,

Max wondered if any of the real Nazis felt this horrible when they met the people of their conquered territories. Surely not all Nazis wore the uniform with pride. Yet neither did they strip it off in shame. Elke's words came back to him: *Most of our fellow Germans made the choice to stand with the Nazis . . . they have made the easy choice.*

Colette beckoned for them to sit at a table made from a rough-hewn slab of wood polished to a fine sheen. She hastily plunked down rolled cloth napkins and silverware. Seated across from Max, Gerta and Kat looked equally miserable. Albert flashed a stern look at each of them in turn, which Max interpreted as a warning—*act like you're proud of yourselves.*

Colette retreated to the kitchen. Through the door, Max could hear the rattling of pots and pans. A moment later Adele bustled over to the table with a bottle of red wine and a handful of glasses clutched by their stems. She poured full glasses for Albert and Mutti, then splashed a little in the remaining three glasses for Max, Gerta, and Kat.

Albert thanked her, then took off his driving gloves and lifted his glass. "*Prost,*" he said. Mutti lifted her glass and repeated the traditional German toast.

Kat gulped her wine down eagerly, made a face, then tried to pretend it had gone smoothly. Gerta pushed her glass across the table toward Max.

"You can have mine," she said wearily. Max left both

glasses untouched. Papa had given him a sip of wine at Christmas, and Max nearly spat it out. He didn't understand how people drank the stuff, and had a suspicion that most grown-ups were just pretending to like it.

He tugged at his collar. He was starving, but would forsake dinner completely if it meant he could go straight upstairs and take off the uniform. He was about to ask if he could be excused when Colette burst through the kitchen door with plates stacked precariously on her arms. She set them down on the table. There was beef stewed in what looked like more red wine and a pile of potato croquettes. Adele came right behind her, dropping off a tray of colorful roasted vegetables.

"Rationing isn't as strict out here in the country as it is in the cities," Albert said in German. "Eat up. It might be the last good meal you'll have for a while."

He speared a big slice of beef and transferred it to his plate. Max did the same, and then scooped up some potatoes, too. He was about to dig in when he spied Colette watching him through the half-open kitchen door. As soon as he caught her eye, she vanished. The heat returned to his face, and when he went back to his food, he found that he'd lost his appetite.

TWELVE

After a troubled sleep, Max's eyes snapped open. His bedroom in the *auberge* was very dark. Albert's measured breathing came from the room's second bed, while Mutti, Gerta, and Kat shared the adjoining room. It took a moment for Max to realize what had torn him from sleep: noises from the inn's first floor, directly underneath the bedroom. Men speaking German, muffled laughter, and then an outburst in French.

Adele, Max thought, sitting up in bed. He held his breath and listened. He couldn't make out the words, but it was clear by the pitch of her voice that she was in distress. Another peal of laughter and a dull thud—the sound of something striking a wall—sent Max out of bed, fumbling in the dark for his knapsack. Quickly, he pulled on his trousers and an undershirt and crept barefoot from the room, shutting the door behind him with a soft *click*. He paused in the corridor.

"This champagne is swill!" one of the German men said. "Bring us something better."

"Maybe she'd like to try it herself?" a second German asked, laughing.

Adele protested in French. Then he heard Colette cry, "*Arrêtez!*"—*stop!*

Max hurried to the top of the stairs and peered over the railing, down into the *auberge*'s front room. Adele was sitting in one of the worn leather chairs. Looming over her were two uniformed SS men. One had his hand clamped down on her shoulder, trapping her in the chair. The other held an open bottle of champagne above her head.

"Open up!" he said, tilting the bottle.

Colette rushed at the man. He struck out with his empty hand and dealt the girl a glancing blow that staggered her. Adele cried out.

Without thinking, Max bounded down the stairs. A red haze obscured the edges of his vision. The champagne bottle paused in its tilt as the soldier turned in surprise. Max hit the bottom of the stairs, sprinted at the man, and knocked the bottle from his hand.

Time slowed. Colette's wide eyes found his.

The bottle shattered, splashing the desk with fizzy liquid. The room erupted into frenzied movement. The soldier took his hand from Adele's shoulder and aimed a wild swing at Max. Adele sprang from the chair, scooped up

Colette, and pulled her toward a corner of the room, out of the fray. Max ducked away from the incoming fist and felt the air whoosh past his face. The smell of alcohol, roasted meat, and sour sweat hung heavily about the soldiers. The second SS man actually *laughed*, harsh and gruff. He moved behind Max, between the leather chairs and the kitchen door.

The man who had swung and missed regained his balance and squared up to face this boy who'd rudely interrupted his evening's sport. He was young and broad-shouldered, blond haired and blue eyed, sprung fully formed from the Nazi mold of Hitler's dreams. Max was breathing hard. As the blond man eyed him with contempt, a smile played at the corners of his lips. Max realized that his drunken sport wasn't ruined, it was just *changed*. There was a new game afoot. The man curled his fingers into fists, then splayed them wide.

"How do you say *stupid boy* in French?" he asked his friend.

"My father's in the Gestapo!" Max blurted out. His perfect native German clearly startled the soldier, who glanced at his friend, puzzled. "He's a *kriminaldirektor* and he's right upstairs and if you know what's good for you you'll leave right now or he'll have you sent to a camp!"

"He's lying," said the soldier standing by the kitchen door.

"He is *German*, though," the first man said. "What are you doing here, boy?"

Reality caught up with Max in a fierce rush—he was an unarmed barefoot boy facing down two drunken SS men with pistols holstered at their sides. He had charged in like Kat with her rocks, and now he was trapped. Out of the corner of his eye, he could see Adele shielding Colette, who peeked out from behind her mother.

"Get out of here," Max said, his voice cracking. "And leave these people alone."

"Go back up to your room, boy, and mind your own business," the SS man said. He swayed slightly on his feet. He was dull-witted and stubborn with drink. There would be no persuading him.

Max glanced at Colette. The only thing to do was double down on his bluff. "The Führer will hear about this," he said.

There was a brief pause. Then the two men burst into braying, uncontrollable laughter. Max realized he'd taken things too far, making an absurd claim.

"Go ahead and tell him, then!" the first man said.

"I'll get him on the phone right now," the second man said, doubling over in laughter.

"Herr Bormann will wake him up for this, surely!"

Max's heart pounded. The situation had become impossible. Who knew how many more Nazis were prowling around this little village? There might be a dozen more of them right outside the front door of the *auberge*. He had put Albert and his entire family in danger, but he couldn't have watched the soldiers torment Adele and Colette from the top of the stairs and crept back to his bedroom without doing anything about it.

And yet what had he really done, in the end?

Here was the price of *brave choices*.

"Step away from my son." The icy command came from the bottom of the stairs. The SS men whirled around. Albert stood there, impeccably dressed, fixing a stony glare on the two soldiers. (Had he slept in his clothes? Max wondered. They weren't even wrinkled.) Albert flashed his silver Gestapo badge in his palm—an eagle holding a wreathed swastika in its talons.

"Your son interfered in SS business," the man said, folding his arms.

"What business is that?" Albert said, glancing at the smashed champagne bottle. "Behaving like animals in this woman's home? We are not Russian dogs. We are *Germans*. The French are our cousins. Act accordingly."

He pocketed his badge and drew himself up to his full imposing height. Max never ceased to be amazed at how Albert could radiate authority as if it were activated by a switch he could flip on and off. "Get out of here. Don't bother these people again."

Chastened, the young soldier gathered up his cap, which had fallen at the foot of the chair. The two men composed their faces into blank masks and headed for the door.

Max let out a breath he hadn't realized he'd been holding. He'd half expected Albert to burst into the room with fists and blades flailing. But of course it was much less dangerous to defuse the situation and maintain their cover.

There was a blur of movement from the corner of the room, and Max turned in time to see Colette step out from behind her mother's back. Her head darted, quick as a snake, toward the first SS man. A huge glob of spit landed on his silver-buttoned breast pocket.

For a moment, nobody moved. Then two things happened at once: the SS man reached for the pistol at his side, and Albert crossed the room in three quick steps, knocking the man's hand away from the holster.

There was to be no more talking. The SS man swung his fist at Albert, who dodged it easily, grabbed the man's arm, and pinned it behind his back, holding him fast. Then he slammed him up against the wall.

Before Max could warn Albert, the second SS man—moving astonishingly fast—drew a small knife from his boot and sank it into Albert's upper back, just below his shoulder blade. Albert grunted, drove an elbow into the second man's face, then slammed the first man's forehead into the wall. Both SS men went down. The one

Colette had spat on lay perfectly still, while the second man cupped his hands around his nose as blood sluiced between his fingers.

Albert delivered a swift, vicious kick to the man's jaw. His head snapped back, and he flopped bonelessly onto the floor.

"Max," Albert said calmly, kneeling and turning his back, "would you mind pulling this out?"

Max blinked. The black handle of the blade protruded from the muscle just to the left of Albert's spine.

"You want me to—"

"Yes," Albert said. "With some urgency, if you wouldn't mind."

As Max steeled himself and reached for the knife, Adele began to usher Colette toward the kitchen door. Albert barked at her in rapid French, and she stopped. Albert explained something that Max could only half understand. Adele and Colette nodded along nervously, then rushed through the swinging door.

"Max," Albert said.

Max gripped the warm hilt of the blade. He thought he'd read somewhere that you weren't supposed to pull a knife from a wound, you were just supposed to leave it alone until a doctor could—

He shook his head. There would be no doctor.

"Steady," Albert said. Max took a deep breath, let it out,

and yanked the knife from Albert's back. It slid out surprisingly smoothly, and then Max found himself holding a knife with a squat little triangle of a blade. There was a small swastika inscribed in the blade near the hilt, the grooves of the Nazi symbol red with blood.

"Thank you," Albert said, getting to his feet. Max handed over the knife and eyed the fallen SS men. They were sprawled on the floor, unconscious. A moment later, Adele and Colette came back into the room carrying cloth napkins and a roll of gauze that unfurled behind them like a parade streamer. Albert gave more commands in French, and Adele began to help him unbutton his shirt.

"Ernst," Albert said as Colette mopped up the blood that leaked from the wound on his bare back, "wake your mother and sisters. Tell them to get dressed and meet me down here. Oh, and pack my things. We're leaving in five minutes."

Colette dropped one of the blood-soaked napkins to the floor and pressed a second to Albert's back. A wave of dizziness almost sent Max to his knees, but he managed to keep himself upright. As Colette clamped the cloth to Albert's body, Adele wrapped his chest in gauze, holding the cloth in place.

Max turned to go. Albert began speaking French again. As Max climbed the stairs, he caught the words *make them disappear.*

He opened the door to the adjoining room to find Mutti, Gerta, and Kat wide awake, their bedside lamp casting a dim glow on their pale, questioning faces.

"Max!" Mutti whispered. "What's going on? We heard noises."

"There was a fight downstairs," Max said, the words tumbling out in a rush. "Albert says to get ready; we're leaving in five minutes."

"A fight with who?" Gerta said.

"The SS," Max said. That sent them all scrambling for their bags and clothes. Max went through the door to his own room, lit the lamp, changed quickly into his Hitler Youth outfit, and then went around gathering Albert's things and packing them up. It struck him that the SS men were just knocked out, not dead—they could come to at any moment. So how did Albert propose to *make them disappear?*

When Max came back downstairs, the two German soldiers were nowhere to be seen. Colette was mopping up blood near the front door. It couldn't be Albert's—he'd been kneeling down in the center of the room.

Colette met his eyes. Max decided he didn't want to know. She nodded slightly, then went back to her task.

Max handed Albert a fresh shirt. Adele helped him put it on, button it up, and tuck it in. Then Max helped him with his jacket. Albert winced a little when he moved his left arm, but other than that, he looked miraculously like a well-scrubbed, well-rested Gestapo agent.

Colette rose, bundled up the bloody cloth, and hurried into the kitchen. Mutti, Gerta, and Kat joined them a moment later, their eyes scanning the front room of the *auberge* for signs of the struggle.

Albert faced Adele and spoke French. She listened, thanked him in French, then said goodbye. Colette peeked out from behind the kitchen door. She looked right at Max.

"*Au revoir,*" she said.

He returned the French farewell, and then she was gone.

Albert turned to Mutti, and she gave him a quick appraisal. "You're hurt," she said. Max wondered how she could tell. Maybe Albert was slightly paler than normal, but other than that he looked fine.

"It's nothing," Albert said. "A scratch."

"Let me take a look," Mutti said.

"There's no time."

Max turned away as a wave of nausea roiled his stomach. When he had pulled the knife out, the flesh at the edges of the wound puckered a bit, then wept like an eye . . .

A scratch. How painful it must be!

Albert went to the front door, opened it just a little, and peered outside. From what Max could see through the narrow opening, it was still dark. After a moment, Albert beckoned for the Hoffmanns and Kat to follow him.

Max glanced back, but the kitchen door was closed and Colette was gone.

Outside, a thin band of dawn was breaking over the gabled rooftops. The village seemed to cascade down from a higher place, where it vanished into darkly wooded hills. A light breeze floated by. The only sounds were the stream that burbled through the shallow stone canal and the low murmur of unseen crickets.

Max followed Albert to the Škoda, which was squeezed into a narrow lane alongside the *auberge*. They took their places inside the car—Mutti up front, Max in back between Gerta and Kat—and Albert held down the starter and then eased the car out onto the cobbled street. As they bumped along, Max kept an eye out the back window for headlights, but no one pursued them.

"What's going to happen to Adele and Colette?" he asked.

"They will be questioned," Albert said, "along with the rest of the village, about the disappearance of those men."

Questioned, Max thought. He wondered if Papa was being *questioned* back in Berlin.

"My father told me that when the Czechs killed Heydrich in Prague," Kat said, "Hitler ordered everybody in a single village killed and then had the village burned to the ground as punishment."

Hitler. Max's thoughts careened to Claus von Stauffenberg, acid fuses, briefcase bombs . . .

Would they ever know what had really happened at the Wolf's Lair?

Albert pulled out of the village and onto the main road toward Paris. Despite leaving the cobblestones behind, the Škoda still bounced along—this road was much less smooth than the Reichsautobahn. It seemed to be made from packed earth rather than pavement.

"Two drunken SS goons are hardly Reinhard Heydrich," Albert said. Max remembered hearing news of Heydrich's assassination. He was the high-ranking Nazi known as the "Butcher of Prague," and in 1942 the Czech resistance had managed to kill him while he drove to work one morning. "Besides," Albert continued, "the French know how to act around Germans—they've been occupied for four years now, and they've learned a few tricks along the way. Adele and Colette will be all right."

Something in Albert's voice troubled Max, but he couldn't put his finger on it.

"I wish you'd pull over and let me take a look at your injury," Mutti said. That's when Max realized what was bothering him—Albert's voice had lost some of its *snap*, the bold, crisp command that was part of his Gestapo disguise. How bad was the wound, really?

Albert didn't say anything. He kept both his gloved hands on the wheel, and the Škoda's engine hummed along as the sky brightened to pale, unbroken blue. Gerta curled up next to Max, put her head on his shoulder, and fell asleep. Kat stared out the window. The rolling hills of the French countryside, divided into chessboards of square farm plots, lulled Max into a daze. As the sun climbed in the sky, the morning grew hot and sticky. Max loosened his hated tie. As he tried to force himself to fall asleep, the early-morning hours unspooled in his mind. There was the Nazi with the champagne bottle, the fear in Adele's eyes, the knife in Albert's back. Behind all of it loomed Colette, pretty even with her face twisted into a mask of hatred as she spat on that clean Nazi uniform . . .

Unnerved, Max turned to look out the back windshield. There was no one behind them. He used his tie to mop sweat from his brow and stared out the window. Cracked patches of mud on the side of the road resembled the scales of a snake. Distant farmhouses dotted the landscape, blots of gray stone on green.

He closed his eyes. Albert had dispatched those SS men—slit their throats, Max guessed—and dragged them out of the front room of the *auberge*, all in the time it took Max to get dressed and pack his bag.

He wanted to believe that all the terrible things he'd seen would fade away when they crossed the border into Spain. But now he thought that there was no place in the world where the war couldn't reach him.

THIRTEEN

By mid-morning they were driving through ruins. Max looked out at a train yard, its platforms empty and forlorn, its tracks bending up from the ground, twisted by the devastation of a direct hit. A sign hanging from the roofless frame of a station house said NOISY-LE-SEC. Beyond the station, gutted apartments bared their interiors to the sun.

"We're in one of Paris's eastern suburbs," Albert said, his voice almost a whisper. "We can't drive straight into the city. The Nazis don't allow cars on the streets, and we'd only draw attention to ourselves."

"Did the Nazis do all this?" Gerta asked as they passed a half-collapsed church, its steeple jutting from the wreckage.

"This is courtesy of the Allies," Albert said. "They won't bomb Paris itself—too many nice things—but out here is fair game."

He turned a corner and eased the Škoda toward a large, forbidding two-story building. There was no glass in the windows, and one corner of the building had been sheared off by a blast, but the structure was otherwise intact. Albert steered down an alley that led to a loading dock. Three gaping archways were open to the building's interior, each one wide enough to accommodate a truck. Albert downshifted, moving his arm with substantial effort, and guided the Škoda through one of the archways. They were plunged into darkness, and Max realized just how sundrenched the morning had been. When his eyes adjusted, he found that they were moving across a vast expanse of abandoned machinery coated in dust. Massive rows of overturned shelves had spilled what looked like bits of leather across the floor.

"A shoe factory," Kat guessed.

"I believe you're right," Mutti said. "Albert?" When he failed to answer, she raised her voice in alarm. "*Albert?*"

The car crept along ceaselessly. Albert's hands had fallen into his lap, and his head lolled against the back of the seat. Mutti slid over, grabbed the wheel, and hit the brakes. The car jolted to a stop. She cut the engine. Wordlessly, everyone scrambled out of the car and went to the driver's-side door. Mutti reached inside, slipped Albert's arm over her shoulder, and pulled him out of the car, staggering under his weight. Together, Mutti, Max, Gerta, and Kat were able to sit him down gently on the dirty floor of the bombed-out factory.

"He's breathing," Mutti said. She pulled her hand away from his back and found that it was soaked in blood. "Help me get his jacket and shirt off." After an awkward struggle with his clothing, they laid him down on his stomach. The white cloth Adele and Colette had applied to his wound was red and sodden. Mutti sucked air through her teeth and glanced around in despair. "Look at this place! There's nothing we can do for him here." She met Max's eyes. "He wouldn't stop driving, Maxi."

"I know," Max said.

Suddenly, a woman's voice came from the darkness at the far end of the factory floor. "You're early!"

The strange accent rang familiar in Max's ears. The woman stepped out from the shadows, trailed by a pair of men, all three of them carrying rifles slung over their shoulders.

She was wearing a brown skirt that hung just past her knees and a collared white shirt with the sleeves rolled to her elbows. It was a radically different outfit than the elegant, urbane clothes she favored in Berlin, but the woman was unmistakably Princess Marie Vasiliev.

Max was struck dumb by the sight of the woman he'd assumed was gone from his life forever, lost to the mad whims of the war . . .

She stopped short when she saw Albert's prone body, then rushed to his side, knelt, and set the rifle down next to her.

"Dear God, what happened to him?"

"He got stabbed in a fight with the SS," Max said.

She reached for her gun.

"Not here," Max said. "In a little village a couple hours away."

"A couple *hours*?" the princess said.

"He wouldn't let me stop or take a look at him," Mutti said. "Not that there's much of anything I could have done. He needs to be taken to a hospital. He's lost a lot of blood."

"Of course he wouldn't stop," the princess muttered. "Stubborn old fool." She glanced around at the gathered Hoffmanns. "We can't risk bringing him to the public hospital, but we may be able to get a doctor to come out here. It's someone we've used before who's sympathetic to the cause. He'll do what he can and keep his mouth shut."

The cause, Max thought. So after the demise of the Becker Circle, the princess had fled to Paris and joined the French resistance. Traded aristocratic fashion for homespun clothes and a rifle. He watched in a sort of awe as she turned to one of the men behind her.

"Henri," she said, and then continued in halting French. Henri nodded and rushed off into the shadows. A moment later, he emerged on a bicycle, zipping past them without a word and vanishing through one of the archways.

The princess watched him go, then turned to give Mutti a quick peck on each cheek. "It's wonderful to see you again, despite the circumstances." She smiled at Kat. "You must be General Vogel's daughter. I was a great admirer of your father. He was a brave man. And he loved champagne almost as much as I do."

"Kat," Gerta said, "this is Princess Marie Vasiliev."

Kat's eyes widened. "Are you really a princess?"

"Forget all that," the princess said. "Just 'Marie' will do, if you please."

"She really is a princess," Gerta whispered to Kat.

Albert's body twitched. A low moan escaped his lips.

The princess muttered a stream of what Max assumed to be curses, in what Max assumed to be Russian. Then she put her hands on her hips and thought for a moment before turning to the second man standing behind her.

"Louis," she said, and they commenced an animated conversation in French. Max picked up the word for *doctor* and not much else, but it was clear by the emphatic way Louis was responding that he was not happy about whatever the princess was proposing. Finally, he threw up his hands in defeat, pulled his peaked cap down low in a gesture of spite, and stalked off into the shadows of the factory.

"Louis will stay with Albert until Henri gets back with

the doctor," she told the Hoffmanns and Kat. "If you follow me, I'll take you to the safe house."

Max looked from Albert's prone body, with its blood-soaked cloth stuck to the flesh of his back, to the princess. "We're just going to leave him here?"

"With Louis," the princess said firmly. "There's nothing else we can do. And this is the perfect time to head into Paris—there are plenty of people out and about."

Max recalled the demolished train station a few blocks from the factory. And Albert had told them that cars weren't allowed on the streets of Paris. "How are we going to get there?"

At that moment, Louis reappeared from the shadows carrying a bucket that sloshed water and a clean white cloth. He knelt next to Albert, peeled off the napkin from his back, and set to work cleaning the wound. Gerta and Kat watched in fascination. Max wanted to turn away. Despite everything he had seen since the strange man had staggered into the Dahlem villa to die on the Hoffmanns' kitchen table—the devastation of the ruined bomb shelter, the swift dispatching of the Gestapo agents at the opera house—the sight of blood could still make him go weak in the knees.

And yet he forced himself to watch as Louis dipped the fresh cloth in the bucket and swiped at the blood on Albert's back. This could very well be the last he ever saw of the enigmatic man who'd saved his life over and over again. He wondered how many other families like the Hoffmanns Albert had dedicated himself to helping survive the war. The man who Max had at first taken to be Frau Becker's butler had turned out to be the linchpin of an entire anti-Nazi crusade, from aiding Jewish refugees to taking direct action on behalf of Max and his family. Not to mention removing several Nazis from the earth—permanently.

Besides Colonel Stauffenberg, Albert was the most courageous man that Max knew.

"Max," Mutti said, "we shouldn't linger."

"Coming," Max said. He reached into his bag and retrieved the wooden knight on horseback. He set it down on the floor next to Albert and nudged Louis. The man paused in his ministrations and furrowed his brow.

"A gift," Max said, pointing to the knight. "For when he wakes up."

Louis nodded. Max hoped he understood. Then he turned and joined the rest of his family as they followed the princess into the shadows.

FOURTEEN

The bicycles were leaning against the wall, just beyond the reach of a long patch of sunlight that came through an upper window. Max counted eight of them. Each bike had a small license plate fixed to the back of its seat.

"This is how Parisians get around under the Nazi occupation," the princess explained. "In the middle of the day, the streets will be full of bicycle traffic. We can blend right in."

Mutti put her hand on Max's shoulder. She didn't say a word, but Max knew what she was thinking. In the last year before the war, Papa had taught Max to ride a bike—the same old bike his father had given him, Papa said. He'd trotted up and down their street in Dahlem while Max wobbled, fell, and got back up to do it all over again. Papa had patched Max's skinned knees and elbows for an entire week until finally something clicked. Mutti had been watching from the front porch when Max returned from his maiden voyage unscathed. He kept riding the rickety old thing until Christmas, when he woke to find a brand-new bicycle gleaming in the winter sun that dazzled the villa's sitting room.

"Now, in the name of all that is holy, change out of those horrid clothes," the princess said. "You can leave them here, but hold on to your ID cards. Hitler sent over a whole gaggle of German citizens to help colonize Paris, and plenty of them still live here. If we get stopped, you won't seem that out of the ordinary." She paused. "Hopefully."

Max found a private place behind a dusty shelf and shed his Hitler Youth uniform. He found a clean shirt, which he rolled up to the elbows, and a pair of loose-fitting trousers perfect for cycling. Then he rejoined his family and tossed his Nazi disguise in a pile with Gerta's and Kat's League of German Girls outfits.

"Good riddance," Kat said. Max watched as she selected one of the bicycles, hopped onto the seat, and pedaled off across the floor of the factory. She was a little unsteady at first, but quickly righted herself, steered into a sharp turn, and sped straight at Max, squeezing the brakes at the last second and kicking up dirt as she skidded to a halt. "I'll take this one," she said.

A moment later they had all chosen their bicycles.

Max was surprised at how quickly riding came back to him—how to balance without really thinking about it, how to lightly pinch the brakes to slow down and squeeze them to stop.

With one last look back at Albert—and Louis standing watch—Max followed the princess out of the factory archway and into the brightness of Noisy-le-Sec.

"Stay close," the princess called back over her shoulder. "And when you see me dismount, be quick to do the same—we'll have to walk our bikes over some of the rubble."

As soon as they left the loading dock, the princess led them down a narrow street past ruined facades painted with symbols that resembled the Christian cross with an extra horizontal line: ╪.

"What's that?" Max asked the princess.

"The cross of Lorraine," she said. "The symbol of the French resistance. Kids like you paint them faster than the Germans can get rid of them."

The princess slid expertly to a halt and dismounted to walk her bike over a low stone wall that had crumbled out into the street. Here, an old man was sweeping a little area in front of a ragged apartment block. He tipped his hat at the princess and Mutti, then continued with his strange, futile task.

Max walked his bike through the wreckage and hopped

back on when the street was clear. They traveled through Noisy-le-Sec until they came to the edge of the deserted train yard, far to the west of where they'd encountered it on the way in. Here, there was no bombed-out station, just rows of forlorn tracks to nowhere, pitted with holes. It looked as if a giant child had torn up his toy railroad in a fit of rage. A black-winged bird perched atop one track that had been twisted into a crooked spire.

They crossed a bridge over the yard, which deposited them onto a long, straight avenue that ran alongside a fetid canal. Small boats lashed to posts bobbed in the listless current. There was more bicycle traffic here, most of it headed in the same direction—men and women hunched over their handlebars, zipping past Max and his family. The smell of sewage drifted up from the water, and Max tried to hold his breath. But the canal and the road just kept on going. Eventually he was forced to gasp for air and abandoned that idea. Finally, they veered away from the canal, and the ruins of Noisy-le-Sec were behind them.

Sweat stung his eyes, and he swiped a hand across his brow. It was very hot. Perhaps it was just his imagination, but the heat felt *thicker* here than in Berlin. His bag clung wetly to his back as he pedaled hard to keep up with his sister. She was a much better cyclist than he was, it turned out.

Gradually, everything began to seem *bigger*. The road

widened, the cobblestones grew smoother, and the traffic picked up so that Max began to feel hemmed in. If he kicked a leg out to one side, he could send another cyclist sprawling and probably start a massive pileup. Grand, undamaged buildings lined the streets, and snatches of city life fluttered past Max's face like ribbons on the wind—shouts, laughter, music.

They came to the edge of a park, where the street split into cobblestone lanes and small canals cut through the greenery in neat tributaries.

Here, he caught his first glimpse of the occupying force: a row of parked Wehrmacht trucks with canvas coverings. Outside the trucks, soldiers in uniform milled about. They looked to be on the older side, and Max remembered Albert telling him that the youngest and strongest had already been sent east to fight the Russians.

To Max's surprise, the princess led them right past the Germans. A group of what appeared to be street urchins in dirty clothes were huddled together in front of one of the trucks. Max caught the eye of a boy about his age as he passed, and then the boy looked away. The kids didn't appear to be miserable or scared, but they weren't smiling, either. He wondered if these were some of the kids who painted the cross of Lorraine on the sides of buildings.

They turned into the park, where bicycle traffic thinned out a bit, and followed a wide canal past amusement booths and a carousel that, to Max's astonishment, was actually running.

This was a very strange enemy occupation.

A few minutes later, they reached a place where two canals crossed. The princess dismounted on a small footbridge. A beautiful apartment building curved along the water, following the natural bulge of the canal. With its balconies and its smooth whitewashed stone, it looked as if it thumbed its nose at the very idea of war. Alongside the canal were wrought-iron lampposts looming above the pedestrians and cyclists weaving across an expansive plaza. There was not a car in sight. A few German officers strolled along the banks of the canal, but they didn't seem to be intent on bothering anyone.

The princess turned to face the Hoffmanns and Kat.

"Welcome to occupied Paris. Don't let its pretty face deceive you. Those of us who fight the Nazis here still die for it, just like in Berlin. And just like in Berlin, most people don't fight them at all."

FIFTEEN

The safe house was in the Pigalle neighborhood in northern Paris, a short ride from where they'd entered the city. Pigalle's narrow lanes and small open squares were choked with Parisians on bikes and on foot. The district was a mixture of somber middle-class apartments and strips of bars, bistros, and clubs that seemed to be doing a brisk business in the middle of the afternoon. At many of the outdoor tables, groups of German officers and enlisted men drank coffee and read newspapers. Max felt oddly dislocated. He had expected the occupied city to feel more oppressed, with beaten-down, defeated citizens slinking around in the shadows. But Paris seemed like it was being *shared* by the French and the Germans.

Unlike Berlin, it was spectacularly intact. There were no streets cratered with holes or buildings half-collapsed by bombs. Max didn't see a single fire brigade rushing to put out the latest inferno or pump air into the rubble of a shelter for the nearly dead to breathe.

Following the princess, Max walked his bike past a building with a stunning red windmill perched on top of it. The sign said MOULIN ROUGE, and posters in both French and German advertised cabaret shows with dancers in outrageous costumes. In fact, there were so many German signs—street signs, store awnings, posters of captured resistance members, propaganda featuring noble illustrations of Hitler—that Max thought he could actually navigate Paris. It was as if the occupying army had simply moved in, nudged the Frenchness of the place aside without wholly replacing it, and injected bits of Germany in the gaps.

They skirted the edge of a vast cemetery crowded with mausoleums, tiny houses, and statues. Then they turned down a winding street. A stray cat the color of marmalade slunk up against his leg and then vanished into a basement window. Halfway down the street was an archway cut into the center of an apartment building. Next to the archway was a door marked CONCIERGE. As the princess approached, the door flew open and a short, matronly woman with gray hair pulled back into a severe bun regarded her with arms crossed.

The princess greeted her pleasantly, and the woman glared back for a moment. Then she beckoned for the princess to come over. They had a hushed conversation, and then the princess led Max and the others through the archway into a small, neglected courtyard. Dry brown plants wilted in flowerpots, and vines grew unchecked up the walls and across the cobblestones. A rusty table sat baking in the sun.

"Madame Agee is the nerve center of this building," the princess said.

"She doesn't seem very friendly," Kat remarked.

The princess walked her bicycle to a shaded brick alcove. There were several other bikes there already.

"Concierges like Madame Agee are required to report all new tenants to the Germans," the princess explained. Max watched as she deftly removed a small tube from a clip on her crossbar—a hand pump for bike tires. "She might not be a ray of sunshine, but she tolerates our presence here and even warns us if the Germans are poking around the neighborhood."

She unscrewed a little cap on the bike pump, slid out a tightly rolled piece of paper, and then replaced the pump on the crossbar. Max, Gerta, Kat, and Mutti leaned their bikes against the wall of the alcove and followed the princess inside the building. A zigzagging staircase took them up three floors. Savory cooking smells wafted down the hall. Max wondered if food here was as tightly rationed as in Berlin. It was strange to experience this parallel world of

Nazi rule—a vast, teeming city that *wasn't* Berlin—and then to imagine similar occupations playing out all over Europe, in Amsterdam, Brussels, Vienna . . .

The princess paused at a door, inserted a massive key in the lock, and led them into a two-room apartment that smelled of potent chemicals. The front room was neatly furnished with a small round table, a set of cushioned chairs, a sofa, a handsome desk, and a gilt-framed mirror that looked as though it weighed a ton. The princess went directly to the back room, and Max followed her inside.

Two teenagers, a boy and a girl a few years older than Max and Gerta, sat at a long table that held two machines about the size of typewriters. Max watched as the girl fed a sheet of paper into her machine and turned a hand crank. The paper slid through the machine, squeezed beneath a roller, and came out the other side freshly inked.

"Mimeographs," Mutti said.

"Yes," the princess said. "We print one of the resistance newspapers here. It's not as sophisticated as Herr Trott's old operation, but we make do."

She approached the table and handed the rolled-up paper to the boy.

"*Merci,*" he said. Then he unrolled the paper and carefully wrapped it around the roller on his machine.

"It's a stencil," Gerta said with authority.

"Sure, Miss Mimeograph," Kat said.

"It is!"

"Girls," Mutti said.

Max eyed a stack of finished "newspapers" on a small end table near the door. The print was tiny, and the papers consisted of a single sheet folded in half to create four small pages. He recognized the words in the bold headline: *RISE UP.*

"Go ahead and take one," the princess said. Max grabbed one of the papers. Beneath the headline, there was a drawing of several people in old-time clothes standing atop a barricade of rubble on a Paris street corner, waving a tattered flag.

"The French Revolution," the princess said. "Nice touch, right? Come on—I'll show you where you'll be staying the night."

In the front room, she went to the fireplace and pulled on the upper left corner of the mantel. Like the false bookshelf in the old sisters' sitting room, the mantel swung open. Behind it, the bricks of the "chimney" formed a staircase. As Max followed the princess inside, the stairs became so steep that he had to use his hands to grip the steps above his head and climb as if he were on a rock wall. He lost the light completely for a moment, but then the princess pushed open a square door for them to crawl through. Max found himself in a cramped and gloomy warren of low-ceilinged rooms.

"We're up under the eaves of the building," the princess said. "At one time these were servants' quarters." She led them through an open door into a slightly larger room with several cots pushed up against the walls. The single window was covered by a thin sheet. "Then they were rented to students. Now Madame Agee is letting us use them for a little while before we pick up and move someplace else."

The humid air trapped at the very top of the building reminded Max of the Berlin safe house, where—incredibly—they were all still living until a few days ago. How long had it been since the attempt on Hitler's life? Five days? Six? He had lost track. And now here they were in occupied Paris, hiding out in another stifling room while Papa was back in Berlin, Albert was bleeding on the dirty floor of a shoe factory, and Princess Marie Vasiliev was secreting mimeograph stencils in a bicycle pump for the French resistance.

His head spinning, Max let his bag fall to the floor and sat down heavily on the nearest cot.

"I'm going to scrounge up some food for you," the princess said. "Rationing's not much better than in Berlin, but I know a guy who knows a guy. Sit tight."

With that, the princess left the room beneath the eaves. Mutti went to the window and peeked out around the edge of the sheet.

"Your father and I came to Paris once, before you were

born," she said. "Your father was still in medical school—my God, it's so long ago now." She moved away from the window and ran a finger absently along the top of a battered old dresser. "We came to see the museums, but I remember it was springtime, and every day we'd stroll on the banks of the river, just to be outside . . ." She smiled, lost in the memory. "I don't think we saw a single painting the whole time we were here." She went to the cot she had chosen and busied herself with the contents of her bag, spreading her clothes on the cot, shaking out and then refolding her garments.

Max scanned the resistance newspaper. He found that he could translate about half of the main article, which he read with mounting excitement.

"Hey, this is asking citizens of Paris to start fighting the Nazis," he said.

Kat snorted. "A little late for that, don't you think?"

"Wait till I tell you why," Max said, looking around the room, savoring the moment.

"Out with it, Maxi," Gerta said.

He tapped the newspaper. "It says the Allies are almost here. It says they could be in Paris in a week!"

SIXTEEN

A week is a bit of an exaggeration," the princess admitted. She had returned a few hours later with a small basket of fresh fruit to find the Hoffmanns eager to talk to her about the article's claims. "It's probably going to be more like a month. Or two."

"But they're definitely coming!" Kat said.

"We certainly hope so," the princess said. "Of course"— she hesitated—"there's a chance they'll just go around."

"*Go around?*" Gerta said, selecting a ripe apple from the basket.

The princess sighed and sat down on a cot. "It's a complicated situation here. The Germans are under Hitler's orders not to destroy anything. He wants Paris to be the jewel of the Reich. And the Allies won't touch it, either—the only bombs that fall on Paris are complete accidents. So nobody's really sure if the Allies are going to bother with the city at all. They could always just march around it, head for Berlin, and wait for the Germans in Paris to surrender when it's clear that Hitler's been defeated." She paused. "Or they could send a thousand American tanks into Paris to take it back street by street. The resistance is hoping to send a message to the Allies by rising up—we're here, we're armed, we're going to fight alongside you."

Max considered this for a moment. He looked at his sister, then met Kat's eyes, where he noticed a familiar gleam. He hadn't seen that look on her face since they'd formed the Red Dragons, and he felt a surge of excitement, as if he'd just launched a rock through the Hitler Youth headquarters' window.

"We could stay in Paris," Max said, turning to his mother.

"That's what I was thinking!" Kat said. "If the Allies are going to be here soon—"

"Absolutely not," Mutti said firmly. "We don't even know if they're coming. And if they do, the fighting will be block by block and house by house. Paris is not a safe place for us to be." She looked pointedly at the princess. "It would be foolish to stay here."

"Wise words," the princess said. "The coming weeks could be devastating ones for Paris. Hitler will be desperate with the Allies on Germany's doorstep. There are rumors that he's going to order Paris burned to the ground if the Wehrmacht is forced to retreat from the city."

Max imagined the glorious French capital flattened into ash and rubble, like Hamburg and Frankfurt, all on the orders of one frightened, cornered man. He leaped from his cot in frustration.

"Why didn't Colonel Stauffenberg just shoot him!?" he fumed. "Then none of this would have happened, we'd still be in Berlin, and Papa would be with us."

"Max," the princess said, "none of us knows what really happened at the Wolf's Lair. We may never know how old Adolf survived the bomb. But we do know that Colonel Stauffenberg was the only one of us who was in a position to kill Hitler. For a man like that, both capable and willing . . ." She shook her head. "I trust that he did everything in his power."

Max felt chastened. "I'm sorry. You're right." He thought for a moment. "I'm just sick of feeling like I'm hiding and running away when other people are still fighting. It's not what Colonel Stauffenberg would want."

"Colonel Stauffenberg would want you to *live*," Mutti said.

"I'm staying in Paris," Kat announced abruptly.

"Kat Vogel!" Mutti said. "Your father—"

"Is dead," Kat interjected. "And my mother's in Ravensbrück. So I'm going to tell the Allies in person that they'd better be going there, to the camp, to get the prisoners out." She turned to the princess. "I'm *staying*."

The princess raised an eyebrow. Mutti folded her arms. "Kat," she said, "I'm responsible for your safety. I can't pass that responsibility on to someone else."

"I'm a good fighter," Kat said to the princess.

"It's true," Gerta said. "Just give her a rock."

"We could always use an extra pair of hands," the princess said hesitantly. "The resistance isn't in the business of turning down volunteers."

Max expected his mother to argue. Instead, she went again to the window and peeked out at the courtyard with her arms crossed. "I consider you part of this family now," she said after a moment. "But tell me, Kat—if I forbid it, if I insist that you come with us to Spain, will you simply run off and join the French resistance?"

"Probably," Kat said, biting into an apple.

Mutti sighed and turned back to the room. "Then if Marie thinks she can accommodate you . . ."

"I'll watch out for her, Ingrid."

Max watched curiously as his sister rummaged through her pack and came up with a crumpled piece of paper. At first he thought it was one of Petra's folded creations, but then she handed the paper to Kat, who smoothed it out and grinned.

It was the calling card of the Red Dragons.

"For the establishment of the Paris branch of Berlin's famous Hitler Youth hunters," Gerta said.

The princess made a sour face. "There are plenty of Nazi kids kicking around Paris, too, unfortunately. The Jeune Front, they're called. Nasty crowd."

Kat pocketed the Red Dragons card. Then she pulled Gerta in for a long embrace. "Don't forget about me when you're getting tan and happy in Spain."

"Oh, Kat," Gerta said, "I'm gonna miss sharing tiny rooms with you."

The princess laughed. "You've still got the entire night to be cooped up together in *these* tiny rooms. I'll be back in the morning. We'll leave here at eight and blend in with the morning rush. Till then—*au revoir.*"

The princess grabbed an apple and left the room.

The air felt immediately thicker in her absence. They fell silent, all of them bearing the weight of Kat's decision. They would pass the time together in these dusty rooms beneath the eaves, low ceiling pressing down, until it came time to say goodbye to Kat.

She went to the window and tapped out a light rhythm on the sill. Max watched her twig-thin limbs and remembered when she had first come to live with the Hoffmanns in the safe house. He'd never known the right thing to say to this girl who bore the raw pain of loss. But things had softened between them over the past few weeks, as Colonel Stauffenberg's doomed assassination plot took shape and then fell apart. Now she was a second sister, and if he didn't always know the right thing to say, it no longer scared him to reach for the words and fail, because he knew that she thought of him as a brother.

He watched Gerta devour her apple with strange ferocity. He knew what his sister was thinking: Would they ever see Kat again? War scattered people like seeds. In just the past few days, Papa and Albert had been blown out of Max's life, and soon Kat would be gone, too. He imagined a postwar journey east, retracing his steps through a hushed and ash-strewn Europe, picking up those he had lost along the way. But he also knew that was a rosy vision of something that would never be so easy.

Mutti crossed the room. She leaned over, mussed his hair, and kissed his forehead. Then she went to Gerta and held her close.

Suddenly, Kat quit tapping the windowsill and spun around. "Okay, Hoffmanns, I should have said this a long time ago, but I'm really sorry. You were nothing but kind to me—you saved my life, taking me in—and I repaid you by sneaking out and getting everybody into trouble"— Max could only watch as the words tumbled out faster and faster—"and this whole trip all I've been thinking is that if I never came to stay with you in the first place, you would all still be together in Berlin, Herr Hoffmann, too, and then maybe Albert wouldn't be . . . wouldn't be . . ." Tears came to her eyes, and she looked away.

Mutti went to Kat, took her by the shoulders, and held her gaze. "Kat Vogel. Listen to me. It has been an honor to have you in our lives. You carry your father's spirit in your heart, and we are all of us blessed to know you."

Kat's lip trembled. "I'm sorry I'm not going with you to Spain, after all you've done for me."

Mutti smiled. "It's quite all right. You stay here with the princess, and when the Allies come rolling in, you find yourself a general and you tell him to get his butt to Ravensbrück."

"You might want to learn how to say that in English," Gerta said, "otherwise he'll just stare at you."

Kat laughed, sniffled, and laughed some more. The air in the room didn't seem quite so heavy anymore.

"I'm not going to tell you goodbye," Max said. Everyone looked at him. For a moment, he wavered on the precipice of *you're saying the wrong thing!* But he kept going. "Because I'll see you again in Berlin, as soon as the last Nazi flag is gone." He picked up an apple. "To Frau Becker," he said, and took a big bite.

"To Frau Becker," Kat said, lifting her apple core into the air. "To Claus von Stauffenberg. And to Ingrid, Karl, Max, and Gerta Hoffmann. See you after the war."

SEVENTEEN

The freight train marshaling yard was several long blocks east of the Pigalle safe house. They left their bikes in the courtyard and joined the throng of Parisians making their way to work on foot during the morning rush hour. As they moved swiftly beneath an overcast sky, the princess explained the next leg of their journey.

"The train will be carrying bags of mail south through the occupied zone. You'll be riding in the second-to-last car—the mail bound for Saint-Jean-de-Luz, a village just over the Pyrenees Mountains from Spain. When you get there, a man named Benat will be at the station to unload the village's mail. He works with us, and he knows you're coming. He'll take you to a house in the village where you'll get ready to go over the mountains. Benat will be your guide. Tomorrow morning, you'll be in Spain."

Max's body tingled at the princess's words. *Over the*

mountains. It was like something out of Grimms' fairy tales. He imagined a treacherous mountain path, gnarled staff in hand, otherworldly birds circling the treetops.

"We don't have—" Mutti began, then abruptly fell silent as they passed a trio of Wehrmacht officers headed in the opposite direction.

"It's okay," the princess said. "Just like in Berlin, it's not really the ones in the army uniforms you have to worry about. It's the Gestapo who hunt us."

"We don't have money to pay the guide," Mutti said.

"Oh, he does it for free," the princess said. "He's Basque, and his people have lived in the mountain regions between France and Spain for centuries. They stick their thumbs in the Nazis' eyes by helping us get people—mostly downed British pilots—across the border." She paused. "Fascinating crowd. They do it for fun, I think."

Max glanced over at the princess as he struggled to keep up the pace on the busy street. One part of him wanted to soak up as much of the Parisian atmosphere as he could—who knew when he would be back in the grand city, and who knew if it would ever be this grand again? But another part of him was entranced by the princess. Even as she spoke, her eyes swept the crowd ahead, darting this way and that, searching for something . . .

"Follow me," she said.

Several things happened at once. Max followed her gaze

to an older teenage boy sitting on a bench, reading a book. The boy nudged a middle-aged man next to him, who got up with a newspaper under his arm, trailed by a pretty young woman. The three of them moved toward the princess and the Hoffmanns, quickly overtaking them and falling in alongside—but just for a moment, because they were soon joined by a portly man in a jaunty hat. As soon as this fourth stranger was close, the princess led the Hoffmanns straight toward the edge of the boulevard. It turned out that this section of the street was actually an overpass, with four train tracks passing beneath.

"Quickly!" the princess said. And then, to Max's astonishment, she swung over the side of the railing and gripped the sides of a ladder that led down to the edge of the tracks. He couldn't believe they were doing this on a crowded street in the middle of the morning. As Gerta swung down after the princess, his eyes searched the street for Nazis. But then he realized the purpose of the other "pedestrians." The four strangers he'd noticed, plus a few others, were loitering in what looked like a haphazard way, while actually blocking the view of the ladder from the street.

"Max," Mutti said, "go!"

Max climbed atop the rail, placed one foot on the first rung, and held the sides of the ladder and descended. The street disappeared, and a moment later, he was looking straight ahead, underneath the overpass, at the tracks vanishing into a tunnel. He glanced up to see Mutti begin to make her way down, then focused on moving as fast as he could. When he reached the bottom, his feet touched gravel, and he hurried to where the princess and Gerta were crouching in the desolate scrub grass. Above them, the concrete wall was tagged with a faded cross of Lorraine.

He noticed that the princess now had a rifle strapped over her shoulder and guessed that it had been stashed in the grass. Mutti arrived a moment later. Max took a few deep breaths. It hadn't been a long climb, but adrenaline was surging through his body.

"The freight cars are loading up over there," the princess said, pointing down the tracks in the opposite direction of the tunnel. "We'll have to keep an eye out for the gendarmes—French police in brown uniforms. Some love the Nazis and some don't, but they all tend to do what they say. If they catch us here, they'll turn us in or shoot us." She paused. "One more thing before we go. The door on your car won't open until Saint-Jean-de-Luz. When Benat opens it, he'll say *How's the weather in Paris?* in German, the only German words he knows. That's how you'll know it's him."

"What if it's not him?" Gerta asked.

The princess unslung the rifle and handed it to Mutti. "That's what."

Mutti held the rifle, blinking, as if it were an alien

object. She opened her mouth, then thought better of it and slung the weapon over her shoulder without a word.

"Stay low and follow me," the princess said, slinking along the wall in a crouch. Max's head spun. It was not yet mid-morning and the air was already sticky with that special Paris heat that glued his shirt to his back. High above, the city thrummed—the hustle and bustle drifted down and swept through the concrete valley in a low murmur. The coarse scrub grass thickened, and wispy branches snapped at his face. They rounded a bend and two idle freight trains came into view, boxcars snaking off into the distance. As they approached, Max noted a few gendarmes milling about, pistols holstered, along with a work crew hauling overstuffed bags and tossing them up through the open doors of the train cars. He also noted that each car was emblazoned with a swastika.

Suddenly, the princess hissed, "Get down!"

Max flattened himself out. The foliage was thicker here, but still full of gaps. It was hardly a worthy hiding place. A pair of gendarmes began poking idly around the nearest boxcar, shining a light into the dark interior, sweeping the beam across piles of stuffed burlap sacks. A workman came up to them, mailbag balanced on one broad shoulder, and said something clipped and loud in French. The gendarmes laughed and moved on down the row.

"Okay," the princess whispered. They made their way

down the length of the train, trailing behind the gendarmes performing their inspection. The boxcars varied slightly in color, from dusky crimson to drab olive green, but they all featured a bright, freshly painted swastika glaring out from the faded slats. Finally, the gendarmes rounded the last car and headed for the second freight train. The princess once again called a halt. She pointed to the second-to-last car. The sliding door was wide open.

"There's your chariot. When I tell you to go, run as fast as you can, get inside, and duck down behind the mailbags. Somebody will be along to shut the doors in a few minutes, and then you'll be off." The princess turned and knelt facing the Hoffmanns. "It's up to you what to do and where to go after the war, and I wouldn't blame you for wanting to go home. But I can't help thinking that Germany doesn't deserve you." She glanced at the train and waited a moment. "Now *go*."

Mutti led the way across the gravel to the tracks with Gerta at her heels. Max brought up the rear, eyes shifting from side to side as he ran, searching for a glimpse of a brown uniform. They crossed the short distance in half a minute. Mutti put her hand on the narrow ledge just below the open door and prepared to hoist herself up—

And then a man came out of nowhere. Or, as Max realized a second too late, from the space between the cars, where they were connected by a steel joiner. A workman's cap perched atop his bullet-shaped head. In his hand he held an enormous wrench flecked with rust spots. He froze when he caught sight of Mutti with her hand on the ledge. His eyes scanned the rifle. Then he strode toward them, hefting the wrench.

Max stepped in front of his sister. Mutti fumbled with the gun.

"*Non!*" the man said in a low yet insistent voice. He lifted the wrench so that it pointed into the door of the boxcar. "*Rapidement!*"

Max knew the word: *quickly!* This man was no friend of the Nazis.

"Go!" he said, and Mutti hoisted herself up onto the ledge and then tumbled into the boxcar. Gerta scrambled up after her and held out a hand to help Max up. As soon as he was inside, the workman gave them a crisp nod and slid the door shut behind them.

The boxcar was plunged into darkness. After a moment, Max's eyes adjusted and he was able to make out the piles of mailbags like misshapen, dormant monsters in the thin strips of daylight that came in through the slats. The air in the car was dense and smelled of mildew.

"Back here," Mutti said, sitting down cross-legged in a little nook formed by a pile of mailbags and the back wall of the boxcar. Max and Gerta joined her on the gritty floor.

"It's strange," Gerta said quietly. "We'll never see that

guy again or know his name. He just helped us, and now we're gone from each other's lives."

"It's people like that who are truly winning the war," Mutti said. "I know things get all jumbled up when we're on the run like this, and it's hard to think straight when we're bouncing from one place to the next and just trying to catch our breath, but there are moments we should try to keep with us. We're going to tell your father the whole story one day, and you know what he always says."

"*A story dies without details*," Max and Gerta said in unison. In the silence that followed, Max thought of his father. What was Berlin like now, in the aftermath of the attempt on Hitler's life? He was ashamed to admit that he was glad he didn't have to find out.

"That could have been it for us back there," Gerta said. "That guy could have yelled for the gendarmes."

"But he didn't," Mutti said, and that was that. How often, Max wondered, had their fate been decided by the whims of a stranger's split-second decision? Probably more than they would ever know.

The car shuddered. The train moved. Soon even his thoughts were drowned out by the *chukka-chukka* rhythm of wheels on tracks, and he said a silent goodbye to Princess Marie Vasiliev and Kat Vogel, two more seeds scattered in his wake. Then he leaned back against a mailbag and tried to get some sleep.

EIGHTEEN

The boxcar door slid open. Mutti was crouched in their nook, rifle trained on the tall, stocky figure that appeared against the darkening sky. They had been traveling for most of the day, and it took all of Max's willpower not to fling himself out the door and into the fresh air of southern France. Instead, he forced himself to hold still. For a moment, the man just stood there, peering into the boxcar. Then he cleared his throat.

"How is the weather in Paris?" he said in halting, garbled German. It sounded as if his mouth was full of pencil shavings. Gerta giggled. Mutti lowered the rifle.

Max replied in French. "*Chaud.*" Hot.

The man sounded relieved as he switched to French. But he spoke too fast, and Max could only catch a few words. He turned to his mother and sister. "It's Benat. He wants us to follow him."

"We got that, Max," Gerta said, rising from her place on

the floor. Benat gestured to someone out of sight. A second man, squat and burly, hopped effortlessly up into the boxcar and shouldered a bag of mail.

Benat reached up to help Max out of the car. His hand was massive and calloused—it felt like a loaf of bread wrapped in sandpaper. Outside it was much cooler than it had been in Paris, and the air was crisp. When all three Hoffmanns were standing in the dirt beside the train tracks, stretching their legs, Max looked up and down the freight yard of Saint-Jean-de-Luz. The tracks were bordered by thick green undergrowth and curious trees with few branches that wore most of their leaves up top like a hat. The small station house flew a Nazi flag. A half dozen workers formed a line, and the burly man began tossing down mailbags from the door of the boxcar, which the others caught and passed along easily. The workers paid the Hoffmanns no mind.

Benat eyed Mutti's rifle and shook his head. The golden late-afternoon light seemed to settle in the deep wrinkles etched into his face. His skin was like a tanned hide, but his eyes twinkled with a spark of mischief beneath the short cap of his beret. He held out his hand, gently but insistently. Mutti unslung the weapon, hesitated for a moment, and then handed it over. Benat led them across a second set of tracks to the tree line. A few paces into the woods, he knelt down, scooped out a shallow dugout with his huge hands, and buried the rifle.

When he stood up, there was a rueful smile on his face. He spoke French again, and this time Max noticed that although he spoke quickly, his accent was strange. *French isn't Benat's first language, either*, he thought.

Benat made them understand that the Nazis patrolled the village, and if they were caught with a weapon, it would be very bad. So they worked their way unarmed through the dense wood. It was quiet except for a chorus of chittering bugs and the occasional scuttle of small creatures. They emerged suddenly on a gentle ridge dotted with shrubbery. A packed-dirt road meandered through the hills toward the white cottages of a small farming village. A single church tower loomed over the houses. At first Max was struck by just how tiny Saint-Jean-de-Luz was. If there were Nazi patrols here, surely they would find Benat and the Hoffmanns in no time! But then his gaze traveled further, and all he could say was:

"Oh."

The farming village was just a stop along the way. The real Saint-Jean-de-Luz unfurled along a vast bend in the French coastline, hundreds of orange-roofed houses cascading down to the horseshoe-shaped beach. Beyond the town itself, the Atlantic Ocean stole pastel hints of dusk from the sky and sparkled all the way to the horizon.

Max had never seen the ocean before. Papa had always promised they would go to the coast one day. *Here I am,*

Papa, he thought. Then he tried to picture the Allies land-ing at Normandy. He imagined the choppy surface speck-led with aircraft carriers, destroyers, landing craft, as far as the eye could see . . .

"It looks like it never ends," Gerta said.

"Not until it hits America," Mutti said.

Max watched his sister stare, openmouthed, until Benat's gentle urging tore them away from the view. They followed their Basque guide down the path until he stopped sud-denly. Max heard the low hum of an automobile engine. Benat beckoned for them to take shelter in the trees along-side the path. A moment later, a Škoda turned a corner and climbed the hill they'd just come down. Max caught a glimpse of the uniformed driver and his two passengers, all three of them SS men.

When the sound of the Škoda faded, Benat led them back out onto the path. Following close behind, Max stud-ied the man's style of dress: oversized dungarees, a sun-faded shirt, and that lopsided beret. He looked very comfortable, and his easy stride helped put Max at ease.

Soon they passed through the farming village. Benat tipped his cap at one or two villagers, but other than that no one paid them any mind. Distant seabirds made great lazy circles above the beach, and the wind carried their cries up into the hills.

Benat led them down a narrow cobblestone street that

curved out of the village, past two rows of trees that grew in perfectly straight lines to form a tunnel of leaves overhead, and into a second village on a bluff overlooking Saint-Jean-de-Luz. They crossed the street. Benat stopped at a neat two-story house, opened a green door, and ushered them inside. An old woman greeted them in broken French and gestured for them to be seated at a rough-hewn wooden table, which had already been set with bowls of stew and hunks of black bread.

Ravenous from his train trip, Max dug in. The stew was delicious. If there was one thing this mad journey west had taught him, it was that food was much better in the country than in the cities. Out here, the natural rhythms of farming defied the Nazis' wartime rationing.

The old woman watched them shovel food into their mouths with bemusement while Benat busied himself in another part of the house. While the old woman cleared their bowls—refusing Mutti's help—Benat dumped a pile of new clothes out onto the floor next to the table. Well, Max thought, not exactly *new*. More like worn, faded garments in the Basque style—dungarees and rough shirts.

"Sleep here," Benat said in French. "Tomorrow, mountains."

Max turned to his mother and sister. "He says we're to sleep here tonight, and then—"

"We got it, Max!" Gerta said.

Benat rummaged in a canvas bag and came up with a set of curious items dangling from his fist by thin coarse rope. They looked like someone's misshapen knitting projects, bits of cloth joined with coils of rope.

He set them on the table. "Alpargatas," he said.

Grinning at the blank looks on the Hoffmanns' faces, he sat down in a chair, kicked off his right boot, then grabbed one of the alpargatas and fastened it deftly around his bare foot, tying the rope around his ankle. Then he looked up, beaming. "Shoe!" he said.

Gerta laughed. "We're crossing the mountains in *those*? I'd be better off in heels."

"Remember what Marie told us," Mutti said. "The Basques have been living here for centuries. If Benat wishes for us to hike to Spain in these . . . shoes, then I think we ought to trust him."

Benat nodded, though Max was pretty sure he didn't understand a word. Then he untied the "shoe," placed it on the table, exchanged a quick word with the old woman, and left the house.

With a smile on her wizened face that was almost apologetic, the old woman pointed up the narrow, winding staircase to the second floor. The Hoffmanns gathered up their packs, their clothes, and their alpargatas, and headed upstairs. There was a small open landing, a bedroom, and a door that led to a second staircase, this one barely wide enough to accommodate them. The old woman insisted with her gestures that they go up, up, up, and the Hoffmanns obeyed, with Mutti in the lead. The topmost room in the house turned out to be an attic with sloped ceilings and a tiny porthole window that looked out upon the sea. There were two thin mattresses on the floor. To Max, it felt like a ship's cabin.

Gerta plunked down on one of the mattresses and sighed. "Looks like we're gonna have to share, Maxi. If you snore, I'll kill you."

Mutti laughed. "Like father, like son."

"I remember I used to come downstairs in the middle of the night for a glass of water, and you'd be on the couch, reading," Max said.

Mutti smiled sadly. "Your father could wake the dead."

Max stretched out on his half of the mattress and rolled up a pair of dungarees to use as a pillow. At first he thought it was ridiculous to try to sleep while it was still light outside. But his belly was full of warm, hearty stew—the best meal he'd eaten in days—and he soon found himself drowsy. The voices of his mother and sister faded to distant echoes, and he was asleep before the sun slipped into the sea.

NINETEEN

Max dreamed of a knight on horseback galloping along the crest of a lonely hill. There was a country churchyard with chipped and weathered gravestones. Try as he might, he could not read the names. Then there was a flutter of paper wings, and he was moving slowly among wondrous creatures. A voice drifted in, calling his name, but he ignored it. He didn't want to leave this place.

"Max."

He turned away from the voice and started to run, but a hand reached out and grabbed his shoulder.

"Max!"

He opened his eyes. It was very dark. Gerta was shaking him awake.

"Get changed. Benat's here. We're leaving now."

Max groaned and sat up. "What time is it?"

"I don't know. The middle of the night. It doesn't matter. We have to go *now*."

Gerta left the room. As soon as she was gone, the sharp crack of a pistol shot sent him scrambling up off the mattress. It sounded like the shot had come from somewhere close, but it was hard to be sure. Footsteps hurried along the street outside. Quickly, Max changed into the shirt and dungarees that Benat had given him. Then he grabbed his knapsack and raced downstairs.

The kitchen was lit by a single candle the old woman had placed on the table, and Benat's massive shadow stalked the walls as he knelt to fasten Mutti's alpargatas, then moved over to Gerta.

Benat glanced over his shoulder as Max arrived and spoke a single word in a low voice: "Nazis."

Max looked at Mutti. "There's a roundup," she said grimly. "I'm not sure if it has anything to do with us, or if it's just bad timing. But the Nazis are on the prowl. From what little I can gather, this village is known for being one of the stops along the network that smuggles downed Allied airmen out of France."

She stood up and paced to the staircase and back to the table, practicing her strides with the strange Basque shoes.

Max sat down, and Benat slid the fabric of the alpargatas over his feet, then deftly tied the ropes around his ankles. The guide spoke quickly and quietly to the old woman in a language that Max didn't recognize.

She bustled around a dark corner of the kitchen, then

returned with an armful of glasses. She set one down in front of each of her guests. Max leaned close to his glass. It was full of white liquid—milk, he guessed, judging by the smell. The old woman gestured with her hands—*drink!*

He watched Gerta down the liquid in one swallow and make a sour face.

"For energy," Benat said, shouldering a small pack.

Mutti drank hers down and wiped her mouth. Max took a deep breath and swallowed the liquid. It was thick and cold, with a strange bite that he felt in his throat, then in his stomach.

"Goat's milk and brandy," Mutti said.

Max felt woozy. Then, despite the urgency of the moment, a mild, calming fog filled his head.

Somewhere outside, the Nazis were shooting. Max counted six *POPs* in rapid succession. Benat eyed the front door. His face, craggy as a cliff in the candlelight, betrayed his anxiety. Max supposed the man had lots of friends in the village, probably involved in the resistance.

They sat, listening in silence, while the old woman gathered up the empty glasses. Engine noise drifted up into the hills from the village proper. There were no more gunshots, but Max could hear shouting in German. The voices, at least, sounded far away.

Benat stood up, put a finger to his lips, and opened the front door. They followed him out into the night.

TWENTY

The Nazi patrol caught up with them in the foothills of the Pyrenees Mountains.

Behind them, the long horseshoe bay was a dark blot at the edge of the sea. Even this far south, French towns were blacked out. Ahead, farm roads curled toward another small village nestled among sparse trees on a hilltop, where neat houses were lightly brushed in moonlight. Benat set a brutal pace, and despite the mild night air, Max was sweating through his dungarees. Sheepdogs barked in the distance. The voices of unseen shepherds called to each other in the Basque tongue.

Suddenly, Max heard an automobile engine. In the pastoral dark, man-made sounds were harsh and unmistakable. The vehicle sounded far away, but Benat ushered them off the road and into the underbrush. Less than a minute later, headlights cut through the darkness and swept across the patch of road where they'd just been walking. A Škoda came roaring into view and skidded to a halt about a hundred meters up the road. Max felt the last bit of the calmness brought on by the brandy milk evaporate. In its wake, his heart pounded.

As he listened to Benat's shallow breathing, his thoughts turned to Hans Meier. The Becker Circle had trusted Hans, and he had betrayed them all. How did the Hoffmanns know that Benat wasn't cut from the same cloth? Their guide could be delivering them straight to the Nazis to save his own skin. They didn't know this man at all—they could barely even communicate with him!

Was it one of those strange wartime coincidences that brought the Nazis to this particular escape route, or had they been betrayed?

Max tried to remember the breathing exercise Papa had taught him to help him relax when his mind began to spin out of control. But trying to recall the technique only made him wish desperately that Papa were here.

Meanwhile, an army truck roared up the road to halt alongside the Škoda.

The two vehicles cut their lights. A dozen dark figures piled out of the truck, moonlight glinting off their rifles. *Soldiers*, Max thought. *Wehrmacht.*

The soldiers divided themselves into smaller squads and began to fan out up and down the road. They clicked on small electric torches attached to their rifles, and thin beams of light pierced the darkness. Benat muttered something under his breath. They were well hidden here in the thick foliage beside the road, but if the search was meticulous, the Germans would find them sooner or later. They could not stay here.

He felt a gentle pressure at the small of his back. Benat whispered *"Follow"* in French. For a brief moment, Max imagined the guide standing up and walking straight out into the midst of the soldiers. Hysteria was gnawing at the edges of his mind, and he almost giggled at the thought of hurling a rock, Kat-like, at the patrol.

Get it together, Max.

Bending impossibly low for such a big, broad-shouldered man, Benat led them away from the road, across a wide, mossy field dotted with lavender. The flowers looked otherworldly in the moonlight. As they embarked upon a steep climb to a tree line that never seemed to get any closer, Max felt like he was barefoot—the alpargatas were durable and lightweight, but the thin fabric didn't provide the support of a good pair of boots. Max felt light-headed. A lucky sweep of a soldier's light would expose them all. He willed the Germans to stay focused on the farm roads.

They were moving uphill in a low crouch, legs pumping in an awkward imitation of running. Max's back began to hurt. He was sure he had never contorted himself into quite this position, and his knapsack just made it worse.

Suddenly, lights stabbed into the night in front of them. The pair of beams were weakened by the distance, but it didn't matter. Gerta couldn't stop her momentum and ran straight through a pool of light as it played along a vivid burst of lavender.

The cries came immediately: "HALT!"

Benat darted off to the right, sprinting nearly parallel to the tree line, and the Hoffmanns followed as best they could. Max could feel adrenaline battle with exhaustion as his legs moved robotically. A web of light closed on them as the soldiers shouted excitedly, zeroing in on their targets.

Benat cut back the other way, and Max nearly slipped trying to negotiate the sharp turn.

The first shot echoed across the field. Max's body tingled, anticipating the bullet. He'd heard that getting shot was like being smashed with a hammer—dull, bruising pain. Then, after the initial shock began to subside, the dreadful searing burn set in . . .

At the sound of the second shot, Benat began to zigzag madly up the incline. Max lost sight of Gerta and Mutti, but their ragged panting assured him that they were close by. His feet plowed through lavender and churned up dirt and moss. His throat felt like it was on fire.

The third shot thudded into the hillside nearby—Max could sense the impact. He risked a glance back over his shoulder and saw a mad scramble of lights. At least ten soldiers were pursuing them up and across the field. Somewhere, a dog barked shrilly.

Just as he thought his lungs would burst, they crested the hill and crashed through the tree line into dense woods. Benat slowed down to allow them a moment to adjust to the new terrain: an overgrown path. Trying to catch his breath, Max looked around for his mother and sister. His heart surged—they were right behind him.

The path wound uphill through dark trees. There was no relief from their ascent, no time to stop and rest. The Germans plodded and crashed clumsily in pursuit. Benat and the Hoffmanns began to outpace them, and the thick foliage swallowed up the soldiers' lights. Still, they could not shake the Germans entirely. Nobody spoke. Nobody had breath to spare.

After what felt like an hour of fighting snapping branches and tripping over gnarled roots, Max noticed a gentle predawn light was making its way across the sky.

Soon it would be morning. Then they would be exposed.

Benat picked up the pace. After another punishing climb, he halted. Max rubbed his tired eyes. Just ahead, the forest path ended at a clearing. The waning moonlight glittered along a muddy expanse. He was aware of the low murmur of rushing water. They had come to a river.

Benat pointed across to the opposite bank. *"Spain,"* he

said. He made a show of rolling up the legs of his dunga-rees. Max, Gerta, and Mutti did the same. Then he held up a hand—*wait here*—and stepped out of the shelter of the forest. He moved swiftly along the riverbank, back and forth, almost all the way to the waterline. *He's making himself a target*, Max realized. It was either a very brave or very foolish way to see if the Germans were in shooting distance. Then, satisfied, Benat beckoned for the Hoffmanns to join him.

Gerta went first, scampering through the muck to the edge of the river. Mutti and Max went next, their alpargatas skimming along the mud without getting bogged down. The sky was a pale orange glow, and the moon had almost faded entirely. The river's current was stronger than Max had imagined, flowing downstream from its source high in the mountains.

Without hesitation, Benat stepped into the water and began to wade across. After a few steps, the water swirled about his knees.

"Okay," Gerta said quietly. She sounded exhausted. "We can do this."

Mutti followed Benat, her steps halting and strange as she quickly sank down to her thighs.

Gerta plunged in after her, and Max brought up the rear. As soon as he stepped into the water, he gasped—it was freezing! In front of him, the water lapped at Gerta's waist, and soon he was equally submerged. His feet struggled to find purchase on the slick rocks of the river-bed. He knew he must stay upright at all costs—one slip and he could easily be washed downstream by the current. He cupped his hands and used them as oars to help propel him along. By the time they were halfway across, the day had brightened, and morning light dappled the river's surface.

Just as his energy began to flag and white spots flashed across his vision, he began to emerge from the water. He took big steps, lifting his knees. They were going to make it! The westward journey flashed before him—the flight from Berlin in the green minna, Elke and Petra's secret room, the *auberge* in the French village, the abandoned shoe factory, Princess Marie's resistance hideout, the freight train, Saint-Jean-de-Luz sparkling along the coast . . .

The rifle shot came from the riverbank behind them.

Mutti cried out and fell sideways into the water. Max's head resounded with a single horrified word: *NO.* Benat spun around, grabbed Mutti by the shirt, and hoisted her up before she could float downstream. Max and Gerta ducked their heads and splashed wildly toward the shore.

The second shot whizzed past Max's ear—he actually *heard* its shrill whiny buzz. Half dragging Mutti through the water, Benat hit the riverbank, slid in the mud, then righted himself. Mutti seemed off-balance but certainly alive as she stumbled along behind Benat, making her way toward the forest on the Spanish side of the river.

Max and Gerta zigzagged through the pebbles and muck at the water's edge as more shots splashed into the river. Then they were up on land and sprinting after Benat and Mutti. Max and his sister both dove for the tree line and tumbled into the forest. There was no path. Max saw sky, leaves, branches, dirt—all of it swirling madly. More shots rang out. He felt a hand clasp his, and then Gerta was helping him to his feet.

"Mutti," he panted.

His mother stepped into view. Max blinked.

"I'm okay," she said, lowering her left shoulder so he could see the gash in her shirt and the angry red wound beneath. "It just grazed me."

Benat cleared his throat and spoke his mangled German as best he could.

"Welcome to Spain."

Gerta threw her arms around him. He seemed surprised as he patted her gently on the back with his enormous hand. Then he led them out of the woods and across rusted and overgrown railroad tracks. They joined a dirt path and descended—how good it felt to walk downhill! As the morning sun dried their clothes, Max fought through sheer exhaustion to a new state of being. He felt as openhearted and expansive as the broad meadows that sloped down toward a shallow valley where smoke curled from the chimney of a stone farmhouse. Mutti walked between Max and his sister and took their hands in hers.

Max couldn't say how, exactly, but he was overcome with the certainty that they would see Papa again one day. He almost said this out loud to Mutti and Gerta, but at the last second he decided to hold his tongue. The feeling would be his alone. It was truer that way, somehow.

As they made their way toward the farmhouse, Max began to smell bacon and eggs.

In the years to come, Max would have plenty of time to live with the story of how he and his family had fought the Nazis and survived the war. For now, it was morning in Spain, and it was time for breakfast.

EPILOGUE

BERLIN, 1945

In the end, Adolf Hitler's assassin turned out to be none other than Adolf Hitler himself. On the afternoon of April 30, 1945, with the Red Army closing in on the Führerbunker, Hitler retired to his personal study and shot himself in the head with his own pistol. His wife, Eva Braun, killed herself with a cyanide capsule. They had been married for less than forty hours.

Germany signed the unconditional surrender on May 8, 1945.

The Hoffmanns, along with millions of other displaced refugees, made their way across war-ravaged Europe and returned to homes they scarcely recognized—if they were still there at all.

The Dahlem villa had been picked clean of everything but the furniture. Even the blankets and candles in the bomb shelter were gone. There was no way of knowing if the culprits were fleeing German soldiers or looters from the Red Army. It didn't matter—the result was the same.

"I can't believe this," Max said, running a finger through the thick dust that had collected on the sitting room end table.

The Hoffmanns had waited out the final year of the war in the Spanish city of San Sebastián. Mutti had found work in the office of a German-speaking dentist, and they lived simply and comfortably. As the months passed, it became easier and easier to put the war out of their minds. In neutral Spain, there were no blackouts, no food rationing, no bombing raids.

No hiding from the Gestapo.

If not for Papa's absence, it would have been possible for Max to let himself be swept pleasantly along by life's new routines. But it had proved impossible to discover anything about Karl Hoffmann's fate in Spain. So, after the war ended, Mutti took Max and Gerta back to Berlin, a city of rubble and ruin, to start life anew in the one place that Karl Hoffmann would return to if he was still alive.

"At least our home is still standing," Mutti said,

straightening a picture frame on the wall. The oil painting of Unter den Linden that had once filled the frame was gone.

"And nobody else is living in it," Gerta said, sitting down on the sofa with a heavy sigh. A cloud of dust erupted into the air around her.

Max went to the doorway of the kitchen. The empty house was eerie in the afternoon light, every corner hiding ghosts, every hallway full of echoes of his father.

There was the wooden table where the man had delivered the maps to Papa before succumbing to his wounds.

Max walked down the hall and peeked into the study. There was the corner of the carpet that hid Papa's safe, the nook in the desk where he kept his doctor's bag, the shelves full of leather-bound medical books and literary tomes.

He could hear Papa's voice, faint and distant: *Max, get me my bag, please.*

He went back into the living room. Mutti was bustling about, straightening up. Gerta sat on the sofa with her arms folded, staring at a torn piece of wallpaper.

This is our house, Max thought to himself. It didn't seem real. He hadn't slept a single night in this place for over a year. He paused for a moment, leaning against the arm of the sofa, thinking about the boy he used to be. That boy, too, seemed unreal.

So who was he, now that the war was over and he was home?

He looked at his sister. She had thrived in Spain, learning the language and making friends easily. Max had mostly kept to himself, despite Mutti's urgings to get out and meet some local kids to play with. He had started keeping a journal, writing down his wartime experiences and memories.

Writing helped chase away the bad dreams. It also helped him stay connected to Kat. Through the few letters that the princess's network managed to smuggle over the border, Max learned that Ravensbrück had been liberated by the Red Army on the same day that Hitler shot himself—and Kat's mother was one of the survivors. They were to be reunited in Berlin.

"Hey, look at this!" he said, noticing a small item on the windowsill. He went over and picked it up. It was a wooden figurine of a knight on horseback—the exact same miniature he'd left at Albert's side as he lay on the floor of the abandoned shoe factory outside Paris.

Mutti and Gerta came over to look.

"Looks like Albert's back, too," Max said.

Gerta made a show of studying an armchair with suspicion. "Albert, is that you?"

Mutti examined the knight and shook her head. "What a strange man."

* * *

Food rationing under the Soviets was scarcely better than it had been under the Nazis, but Mutti could still work magic with the black market. By the end of the week, they had enough food for potato pancakes, schnitzel, and a hearty vegetable stew. They were just sitting down to eat when a knock came at the front door.

Max put down his fork and went to get it. He was expecting one of their neighbors from Dahlem. All week people had been stopping by to say hello and see how they were getting on. Max regarded them all with contempt. Most of them were former Nazis. The end of the war didn't erase their complicity.

He opened the door.

There, with his hat in his hand and spectacles perched on the bridge of his nose, stood a gaunt, hollow-cheeked man in a threadbare coat, standing with the aid of a cane.

Max blinked. The world went askew. For a moment, it seemed that all of Dahlem was fracturing, breaking apart around the figure on the doorstep. Then everything came rushing back together, and a single word escaped him.

"Papa."

Karl Hoffmann fixed a crooked smile to his face. "Max," he said. And then Max found himself half embracing, half dragging his father inside the house while Papa chuckled.

"Careful, there's not as much of me as there used to be."

Mutti and Gerta came rushing over, and in a moment they were all holding one another, afraid to let go. Mutti began to cry as she kissed his forehead, his cheeks, his lips.

Finally, Papa managed to free himself and walk slowly but steadily over to the sofa, the tip of his cane clacking against the floorboards. He leaned the cane against a cushion and sat down. Then he took off his hat. His hair was thin, wispy, and whitish gray. Behind the spectacles, his eyes seemed to stare off into some unfathomable distance. Max knew without having to ask that his father had been in a camp.

"I've missed you so much," Papa said. He took off his spectacles and wiped his eyes. "I didn't know what I'd find when I got here. If the house would be empty. Berlin, it feels like . . ." He shook his head. "It's no longer a city. I don't know what it is. I was afraid our house would be the same way. A tomb. A graveyard of memories." He looked around at his family, and there was great wonder in his expression. "But you're here. You're all really here." Suddenly, his skinny arm darted out and his hand clasped Max's elbow. "Tell me you're really here," he said. His bottom lip trembled and his shoulders shook.

"I'm really here, Papa," Max said. "We're all here. We made it."

Karl Hoffmann wept. "There were times when you were so far away that I thought I dreamed you."

He looked so weak, but his grip on Max's elbow was fierce. At that moment, Max realized that for the Hoffmanns, the war would never really be over. But that was okay, he thought. They were all back home. They had survived. And they would meet whatever came next as a family: Max, Gerta, Mutti, and Papa.

Together.

AUTHOR'S NOTE

Resistance to the Nazis during World War II was a sprawling, international affair that often hinged on the split-second decisions of ordinary men and women willing to make incredible sacrifices. Once I began researching, the rabbit holes proved to be endless, filled with unbelievable characters, wild events, and acts of courage that made me question how I would behave in similar circumstances. (One of my favorite stories, whose events in no way intersect with this series, is the tale of the assassination of Reinhard Heydrich, "the Butcher of Prague," by agents of the Czech resistance who parachuted into the occupied city.)

The treacherous path through Occupied France and across the Pyrenees into the relative "freedom" of Spain really existed. The Comet Line, led by a Belgian woman code-named Dédée, helped hundreds of downed Allied pilots escape the clutches of the Gestapo and live to fight another day. The Hoffmanns' route in this book roughly traces the route of the Comet Line. The final leg, at the French-Spanish border, really was operated by Basque guides whose families had lived in that mountainous region for centuries. Peter Eisner's book *The Freedom Line* was incredibly helpful as I wrote the scenes set in those areas, and I took from it a variety of details, including the all-important alpargatas.

The Nazi occupation of Paris created a weird alternate universe in the middle of war-torn Europe. It was supposed to be a symbol of the Nazis' benevolent power, so rather than bomb it into submission, Hitler settled thousands of German citizens there in an attempt to "colonize" it, while the SS and the Gestapo kept the French population in line. This made for a tense and awkward coexistence between an occupying force trying to refrain from brutality (except against the Jewish population, of course) and a citizenry trying to preserve some semblance of its national character and pride. But not everyone simply went about their business. Resistance groups operated all over the city. In the final days of the occupation, as the Allies drew ever closer, the resistance rose up. (I believe that Kat and the princess fought alongside them, but that's a story for another time . . .) The excellent book *When Paris Went Dark* by Ronald C. Rosbottom helped me bring the characters to occupied Paris.

I would also like to cite Alan Furst's novel *A Hero of*

France for inspiring the Hoffmanns' train journey out of Paris and into southern France.

So much has been written on resistance activities during World War II, and yet countless stories of defiance and sacrifice will no doubt remain forever untold. This series is dedicated to everyone whose acts of resistance went unwitnessed and unrecorded.

ABOUT THE AUTHOR

Andy Marino was born and raised in upstate New York and currently lives in New York City with his wife and two cats. You can visit him at andy-marino.com.